FALL LIKE RAIN

Nell Corbly

Fall like Rain
Nell Corbly

ISBN (Print Edition): 978-1-54399-132-1
ISBN (eBook Edition): 978-1-54399-132-1

Cover design by Madison Rhodes
Illustrations by Nell Corbly

https://store.bookbaby.com/book/Fall-Like-Rain

INTRODUCTION

She thought an internship with an anti-trafficking organization in Cambodia would look good on her resume. American masters student Sophy Seng got far more than she'd bargained for. Her world was rocked when she saw Cambodia through the eyes of a child. A child who was now grown up, but whom she'd never meet.

DEDICATION

This book is dedicated to the people of Cambodia, especially those of you who shared your stories with me. You have patiently encouraged us as we stumbled through learning your language. You have patiently taught us, when were humble enough to learn, about your culture, and endured our sometimes-awful mistakes. And when the time was right, you shared your stories — no matter how hard.

ACKNOWLEDGEMENT

I would like to thank my husband who encouraged me greatly in this endeavor, over the last seven years, and my children (and grandchildren), who have sacrificially and supportively endured a cross-world relationship since they grew up and left their Cambodian home for their original homeland.

And I am grateful for a few friends and family who read the early drafts. You know who you are. Thank you for your time and invaluable feedback. Special thanks to my developmental editor and friend, Janet.

And I thank my God who gave me the amazing opportunity to hear these stories, and whose teachings refresh my heart as they *fall like rain*. (Deuteronomy 32:2)

GLOSSARY OF TERMS

Khmai: the correct pronunciation of the primary people and language of Cambodia (usually seen written in the French spelling, Khmer)

Bong: older person (brother or sister)

B'oan: younger person (brother or sister)

Oan: term of endearment (sweetheart or honey)

Ming: aunt (younger sister of your parent)

Bu: uncle (younger brother of your parent)

Oam: aunt/ uncle (older sibling of your parent)

Yay: grandmother

Da: grandfather

Krama: Cambodian cotton scarf, used for many things from wiping your brow, to shielding from dust and wind, to carrying babies

Bien: large pot for storing water

Preah Put: Buddha

Preah Jesu: Jesus

Preah Ang: god

Wat: temple

Romok: flat uncovered utility cart pulled by a 125cc motorbike (carries people or cargo)

Tuk-tuk: covered passenger cart pulled by a standard 110cc motorbike

Moto: motorbike/moped

Name pronunciations: emphasis on second syllable

Ph = P

Th = T

Kunthea: gun-tee-a

Sopheak: so-pay-uk

Sela: say-la

Mony: mo-nee

Malia: ma-lee-a

Sokaa: so-kaa

Sina: see-naa

Bopha: bo-paa

FALL LIKE RAIN

CHAPTER ONE

December 21, 2016

How is it possible to have learned so much and yet feel smaller and more ignorant than before? This was the question that consumed Sophy, as an endless sea of patch worked rice fields passed beneath the plane.

She was in no mood for small talk. So when two French guys took the middle and aisle seats, she was glad they'd have each other to talk to. And she was glad she did not know French, so their conversation was not a distraction. Like a string quartet of background music for her thoughts, their voices lilted.

With her elbow on the armrest and chin on her hand, she kept her gaze fixed out the small plastic oval window of the 737. Six short months and yet it seemed like a lifetime. Are not these the same rice fields she had seen from the plane in June? The same red clay tile rooftops? Four years of undergraduate school, and closing in on her master's degree, she pondered the possibility of learning more in only six months' time. Tilting her head forward, she let her long silky black hair fall like a shield, a private tunnel for her blurry gaze. Pulling her sleeve over her hand, she quickly wiped the tears from her cheeks, lest they fall and be noticed.

Taking a deep breath in, Sophy thought, *A twenty-four-hour trip is not enough time to process.* Her mind whirled with the images of these past six months: the old worn diary, and the new clean one with only one entry; the curvy Khmai letters dancing through the pages, from shaky childish scribbles to a river of beautiful script; the mugshots of the dead at the genocide museum, faces that looked way too much like herself; her parents, and the final image that was stuck in her memory; a young woman, through a translucent veil of steady rain, dropping to her knees in joyful release; the young woman whom she'd never met and yet grew to know so well; and the young woman who could have been her friend, had they not grown up in different worlds.

When she had flown in, the landscape seemed quaint and serene. But now she knew. The clay roofs had stories to tell. Beautiful stories. Hard stories. Real stories.

"B'oan Srey, druo-gaa bay-sejaec dtay?" The flight attendant woke Sophy out of her thoughts.

"Yes, I'd like a Coke with no ice, thanks," she answered in English.

She flipped her seat tray down and pulled out the diary she'd bought at small fair-trade shop in Phnom Penh. Running her fingers over the smooth blue and gold silk cover, she paused, and she remembered the blue silk skirt that her mother wore to special occasions, like the spring choir concert at school. And she remembered how embarrassed she'd been; the other mothers had worn *normal* dress clothes. Biting her lip and fighting more tears, Sophy wondered if she'd ever know what "normal" was again.

Opening the diary and clicking her pen, she began to write:

"Dear Diary,

I am Sophy Marie Seng. I am 28 years old and I still have a lot to figure out . . ."

CHAPTER TWO

Six months earlier
June 22, 2016

Sophy leaned in against the small plastic window, straining to see more. The 737 dipped below the clouds. She squinted at the bright white reflection from the meandering river bends below. Rectangular patches of land sprawled in every direction. Red clay tile roofs on stilted wooden houses and clusters of sugar palms dotted the landscape. Rain lay puddled in the fields, soaking the soil in hopes of fresh new rice plants.

This last flight from Taipei to Phnom Penh was different than other flights. The Chicago flight was buzzing with loud conversation. "How 'bout those Cubs!", and nothing but mini pretzels to eat. The long flight to Taipei had been more hushed — westerners and Asians hunkered down with their blankets and eye masks, each attempting to defy their claustrophobic spaces and actually sleep. But this last flight into Phnom Penh filled Sophy with a strange dread. She heard bits and pieces of Khmai phrases. Murmurs all around her. Reminders of her heritage. The heritage she had rejected. Sophy had only heard

Khmai in her own home and at family gatherings. She had never heard a stranger speak it.

The woman next to her tried to start a conversation. Suddenly Sophy felt completely inadequate to speak her parents' mother tongue. "Sorry, I don't speak Khmai," she winced a slight lie. Even though she'd heard it all her life, Sophy had refused to speak it since she was five. They would speak to her in Khmai, and she would reply in English. There was much she did understand. But she never learned to read and write the language and had very little confidence to speak it. Why had she agreed to this internship? Even though she felt American, she looked Cambodian, and everyone would try and speak with her.

Her parents had clung to her as if she was never coming back. She'd wondered, once again, why they were always so fearful. At twenty-eight, Sophy was a bit more patient with her parents than she was as a teenager, but many things about them still irked her: the fact that they still did not speak English correctly, that they would not talk about anything important, that they labelled her a "disrespectful child" when she was only trying to be normal, never saying they were proud of her, despite the fact that she got a huge scholarship to Ohio State. And now . . . now that she was going to Cambodia for this internship, they decide to act like they cared? "Don't go out at night. Don't trust anyone. Don't, don't, don't!"

Tall for a woman of Cambodian descent, Sophy stood at five feet seven inches in her bare feet. Her thick black hair fell to the middle of her back. Often, to balance the weight of it, she wore it in a high pony tail or messy bun on top of her head. Wide-set eyes gave her round face a triangular feel. They were almost black, strikingly dark when compared to her pastel-eyed American friends.

The anticipation was overwhelming as the plane landed. She stuffed her Kindle in her backpack and snapped her plush red Ohio State neck pillow onto the top strap. Hoisting the pack onto her back, she stood with one knee on her seat as the plane began to empty. Finally, periscopic suitcase handles clicked into position as her row began to disembark.

"Thank you for flying EVA." The flight attendants smiled and bowed. Sophy noted their polite demeaner and impeccable appearance: black hair pulled into perfect low buns with matching barrettes, and dark green silk scarves tied in perfect knots exactly at the seven o'clock point on their fair-skinned necks. Taiwanese, she suspected. The same dark eyes, but not so almond-round as Khmai, and fairer skinned. Reserved, calm and super polite. Not relaxed, casual and loud like American flight attendants.

Exiting the airport, Sophy felt a blast of dense hot air. August in Ohio can get hot, but this was different. This air was heavy and it hung like an unwanted blanket over her, trapping her in a hard-to-breathe space. Pausing to check her backpack for her phone, she saw her neighbor from the plane mobbed by crying people. Family members, she presumed. Trapped between the hugs and tears, a small boy trembled with confusion and concern. Apparently, he had never met this woman. He looked to be about six, and he shrunk back as the adult voices bombarded him: "It's your aunty from America! Go on and kiss her!" Sophy did not realize she'd stopped to gaze upon this scene. She couldn't take her eyes off the little boy, and she wondered if he felt caught in the middle of two worlds like her. A whistle broke the arrested time.

Sophy scanned the sea of faces. She was not used to seeing all black-haired people. And they all seemed a bit short. Shading her eyes from the intense sunlit background that silhouetted the figures, she spotted a sign, "SOPHY SENG". Seeing her connect with the familiar name, the sign-bearer grinned from ear to ear. He rushed around others to help her with her bags, leaving her nothing to carry but her backpack. To keep up with him, she quickened her step as they weaved in and out of the crowds. She felt a bug run down inside her shirt and winced and wiggled, grabbing at it through her t-shirt. Feeling the damp shirt, Sophy realized it was actually a big drop of sweat.

"My...name...is...Sret." Pointing to himself, he sounded out the phrase as he threw her suitcases in the trunk of an old white Camry. Sophy was relieved that someone had told this guy she was American and he was not stumbled up in the least by her looks.

"My...name...is...Sophy," she parroted his cadence with a friendly smile.

With a big grin, he nodded knowingly. "So-Pee!"

Sophy remembered that she was twenty-eight now, that it was ok if people said "So-Pee" because Pee means nothing in Khmai, so she surrendered on this point, and smiled. Sret was the same height as Sophy. He was stalky and strong with a gentle and kind demeanor. And he seemed to smile continuously. His twinkling black eyes were the kind that smiled on their own, in such a way that made Sophy feel his whole face was smiling. That kind of smile was impossible to not return.

Next thing she knew, Sophy was climbing into bed under a powerful little air-conditioning unit at a quaint garden guesthouse. She'd asked for a bottle of water and an extra pillow. For the first time in her life, she felt grateful that she understood basic Khmai, since no one there seemed to speak English.

CHAPTER THREE

"That is your main focus. The website. And the English classes." Her supervisor was the same age as Sophy. Bethany had been working with Safe Space for nine months. She seemed to enjoy flaunting her knowledge of Khmai culture and anti-trafficking work. Her defences were up with Sophy, and it was only her first day.

Bethany motioned to Sophy and strutted down a hallway, stopping at a doorway. Chunky white Hello Kitty Crocs, shiny blue flats and a variety of dusty leather slip on sandals littered the threshold. "There is a lot of dirt here. Khmai people always take off their shoes before entering a room."

I've only been told that my whole life. Sophy tried to keep from rolling her eyes.

"This is Sophy. I know she looks Khmai but she is actually American, so she really doesn't know anything about Cambodia," Bethany introduced her to the team of Safe Space workers.

A young, neatly dressed Khmai man interpreted for the local staff, while Bethany nodded her head knowingly, "*Ni jia Sof-wee . . .* This is Sophy. She has a Khmai face because her parents are Khmai, so please welcome her to *Gonleing Sovwatapheap* — place of safety."

Sophy smiled as she pondered the difference between what Bethany had said and the interpretation. The local staff smiled and bowed slightly towards her, with their hands together in a praying stance. "Welcome!"

This is going to be interesting.

Sophy had graduated six years earlier with a bachelor's degree in communications. After work stints at two different companies and two failed relationships, she began to ponder the bigger questions of life. To look for something to do that had a longer lasting effect than writing ads for body soap, cars and furniture, she quit working and went back to school for a master's degree in creative writing. Sophy could not articulate how this might lead to meaningful work, but it was at least a step in the right direction. It had been three months earlier when Sophy's favorite professor had approached her after class. "Sophy, your parents are Cambodian; is that right?"

"Yes . . . Why?"

"We have a request for an internship with an anti-trafficking organization in Phnom Penh, Cambodia. I think that is the capital city. Do you speak Cambodian?"

"Well I understand it and speak a little, but I am not that interested in Cambodia." She had blown off the suggestion. Sophy knew she would do an internship as part of her studies and had hoped for a placement in Europe or Australia.

"Well, how about you think about it?" He handed her some paperwork. So here she was, in Cambodia.

It turned out that Sret was Sophy's regular assigned driver through Safe Space. His English consisted of the phrase "My name is Sret," so he was happy to find out that Sophy could converse a bit in

Khmai. Clearly relieved to be speaking his own language, he began to rattle off full sentences. "When I met you I did not even see that you look Khmai," he laughed, "because you did not act like a Khmai!"

"What does that mean?" Sophy struggled with her communication at this point and began to realize that her Khmai was limited. She did not have all the vocabulary to say everything she wanted. And she felt a bit irritated with her stubborn five-year-old self, who'd made a decision to never speak it.

"*Ti Mu-ey, neac dau koh-knia, b'oan srey* . . . First, you walk differently, little sister. Second, you talk differently. And one more thing, your clothes are different . . . very . . . American. *Bundtai, aut ai!* But it's ok! No problem. Mostly, us Khmai people like Americans!" Sret grinned.

"Ah, I see . . ." Sophy laughed off the moment as she wondered who was included in the *mostly* group and who was not.

CHAPTER FOUR

It had been one week, and Sophy was about over jet lag. She went jogging at the riverfront park to help her body get turned around. It was easy to blend in, and no one bothered her, which suited Sophy fine. If you'd ask any of her friends from high school or college, they'd have told you that Sophy was an extrovert. And it was true that she could start a conversation from nothing. She could hold her own in any crowded place and not be intimidated like her more introverted friends. So, none of them believed her when she said she enjoyed her time alone, contesting the label "extrovert". In fact, she was thrilled, as part of her master's studies, to discover the term "ambivert" and claimed it as part of her own identity.

She was pleased to discover that foreign tourists assumed she was Khmai, and Khmai people assumed she was a foreigner. She still did not know what it was about her behavior that made them think this about her. But she liked being left alone at times, or at least being able to choose when to interact.

It was 6:00 a.m., and she pushed through the run to beat the sun. At only 12 degrees north of the equator, she knew it would make her sizzle by 7:00 a.m. Sophy remembered how her friends in high school always tried to get more sun and tan their skin. *They should come here!*

she laughed to herself. They were so jealous that her skin was naturally darker, and all she ever wanted was lighter skin.

The early morning riverfront park of Phnom Penh was a stark revelation of each night before it. A continuous low granite bench stretched the entire length of over one kilometer, dividing the park from the river bank. A peek over the edge revealed various kinds of trash from the night before. The river was neither high nor low, since it was still early in the rainy season. The real monsoon would hit in September. Sophy had heard that the sun still shone every morning, even during the monsoons. A skinny teenage boy with matted long hair squatted on the bench. A greenish plastic bag cupped to his mouth, he sucked in and out as the bag inflated and deflated. Another boy tossed his bag on the river bank and began a loud tirade at no one. She'd heard about teens sniffing glue, but had no idea she'd see them doing it at that early hour in public. It was jarring.

At 6:45 a.m., she slowed to a walking pace to warm down. Wiping the sweat from her neck with her small towel, she sat down on the granite ledge. Her foot hit something, and she looked down. There, hiding in the dark shadow of the bench, was a worn brown fabric satchel-style backpack. She pulled it up to the bench and instinctively looked around for an owner. When no one appeared, she opened the drawstring. Inside were two notebooks. One looked to be quite old and tattered. She leafed through the pages, and it was clear they had travelled far and long. Some had been wet and dried in that crinkled sort of way that wet papers do. The script was Khmai, some in pencil, some in various colors of pen. And it changed throughout the pages. The cover was plastic and appeared to have been pink at one time. Dulled now, blackish English script read "Happiness Memory" in cursive. Sophy shook her head with irritation. *They actually printed this without checking the English!* It gave rise to memories of her parents. The things they said in English. They'd learned enough English to get by, but their grammar was often wrong. *It is hard to gain respect when you do that. Makes you seem simple,* she thought.

Remembering the second notebook, she set the old one down. This one was quite new and sturdy. The front cover read "My Dairy". "*Ugh!* What, like your dairy farm?" she muttered out loud. Most of the pages were empty, and again there was handwritten Khmai script, all in blue pen, for two-and-a-half pages only. It seemed she had found someone's diaries. The first one had run out of pages, so perhaps the new one was a continuation. The writing in the second one was smooth, not childlike, and seemed to match the end of the first one.

Now what to do? She glanced around again to be sure no one around her seemed to be looking for something lost. Not seeing any clues, she tossed the pack onto her own back and began looking for a policeman. Surely, they had a lost and found at the police station. In her first week in country, Sophy had noticed that there were at least two types of police: the ones in white and blue uniforms, and the military police in khaki, most of whom carried larger guns. Sret had told her they were called AK47s. Not finding any police, she glanced across the street at a sign: "The Blue Pumpkin". A giant ice cream cone adorned the text. She'd have thought it was an ice cream shop and thus not yet open for the day had she not seen several people walking in that very moment. *Hmm . . . ice cream for breakfast?* She shrugged.

Standing on the curb, she watched and waited as noisy motos ran over the tall shadow of her own form made by the intense morning sun. There was something about the Cambodian sun that made shadows extra dark. Combined with the rumbling engines, beeping horns and rolling *r*'s of the language, it felt like a dance — patches of light and shadow cut into pieces and leaping around to the local music of everyday life.

Seeing a break in the action, she jogged across the two-lane street, and pulled the glass door open. Not being able to remember the right words in Khmai, she took a gamble on the fact that this was a riverfront shop. Surely the staff would speak English for the tourists.

"I think someone lost this," holding up the bag for clarity, she explained to the waiter in English.

"Yes, very good!" he replied with an enthusiastic grin and a thumbs-up.

Sophy then knew they were not connecting. "Yes, right. Thank you . . . Uh, can I please have a latte?"

CHAPTER FIVE

Sophy wandered upstairs with her hot latte, and was pleasantly surprised by the interior design. Everything was white and bamboo, cool and soothing. This was in sharp contrast to most décor she'd seen so far: the more colors, the better, adorned with gaudy gold. As an American communications major, Sophy had a strong bias towards minimalism in design, so much of what she saw in Cambodia felt like visual assault.

A few foreigners were scattered on giant white couches that lined three sides of the room. The couches dwarfed the people sitting on them, so that, at first glance, they looked like children. Scrolling on smartphone screens, two girls with thick Aussie accents chatted about their flight departure times. Overstuffed backpacks were propped up against the couch front below. Four Teva sandals, which had clearly fallen from above, dotted the floor randomly. Sophy found a seat right by a picture window that looked out over the river. First, she surfed her phone for messages from home. There were about a thousand from her parents. "Are you ok?" "Where are you now?" "Do you have friends?" "Where are you living?" "Is it safe?" "Are you going out at night?"

When her latte was done and she was bored with her phone, Sophy noticed the old brown cloth satchel and sighed. *What to do with this?* She stared out the window and was glad it was Saturday; she had no place to be at 9:00 a.m. The street below began to buzz with activity. Motos pulled on and off the sidewalk, riders parking and entering shops. The garage-style rolling metal gate doors that had been shut when she'd arrived for her run at six were all open now. The sellers had moved racks of wares forward, onto the sidewalks. Two old white men sat at a roadside table at the restaurant below. One of them blew out a puff of smoke and smashed the cigarette into a Tiger Beer ash tray, while the other flirted with the waitress. At the same table, a young Khmai woman dawdled on her smartphone. Her pink flip flop dangled from her foot as she bounced her crossed leg. The waitress walked away and the men chatted, ignoring the girl who was with them. As Sophy pondered that situation, her eyes followed the traffic across the street. Another old white man was walking down the street with a young Khmai girl. His wrinkled skin defied the reddish blonde color of his hair, and she guessed him to be about seventy years old. He wore jeans and sandals, and an Angkor Wat t-shirt that did not hide his beer belly. The girl was holding his hand with one hand and scrolling her phone with the other. She was wearing silver platform sandals and a short tight chartreuse dress. Confused by the scenery, Sophy grabbed her phone to check the time: 9:27 am. She felt a bit sick to her stomach. Sophy thought of the girls at Safe Space. The safehouse currently housed fifteen girls. In her first week, she'd read the profiles of six of the girls. *Is this where it begins?*

Again, her eyes drifted back to the satchel. She took out the old diary and flipped through some pages. Although Sophy could not read Khmai, she could see that, in each entry, there seemed to be numbers and some repeated words — Perhaps a name? She grabbed her phone and searched "Translation services Phnom Penh". About eight titles came up. She touched the first one on her screen. "Lighthouse Publishers and Translation" came up with lots of positive reviews. "Super professional work!" "If you need accuracy, this is the service."

CHAPTER SIX

Sret had said he'd be free at one thirty. So she had time for a shower and some lunch. They drove up and down Street 856 on his moto, at least six times, looking for house number 14. Each time they crossed a road, the house numbers either reversed or started over. They found exactly three houses on Street 856 with the number 14 posted or scribbled in paint on the gate. The last one had a very small sign on the rusty blue metal gate. "Lighthouse" was all it said. The gate was open a crack. It was a *p'teah l'wang*, a typical row house designed for multi-family living and store fronts. The end units were a bit brighter, since they had windows in the front and back, plus the sides. The inside units were a bit cave-like, darker but also cooler. The front room had a high ceiling with a single fan spinning to stir the stagnant air. A young girl was pulling books off the shelves and wiping them off with a damped dirt-stained cloth. Sophy pulled the cotton *krama* from her neck and wiped her face. Seeing the visible dirt streaks she left on the scarf, she surmised that everything needed wiping off in Cambodia.

A thin young Khmai man who looked to be in his early thirties greeted Sophy.

"Hi, I am Phearun." His English was almost perfect. "Can I help you?"

Sophy excitedly pulled out the two notebooks. "I think they are diaries. Maybe one is just a continuation of the other . . . *Bi bru-a, aksaw doit k'nia.*" She surprised herself by finishing the sentence in Khmai. She quickly stated that last part again in English, as if he wouldn't notice. "Because the letters . . . the handwriting looks the same." She sat across his desk, both notebooks open, her fingers pointing at the Khmai letters in each, and looked up at him.

He burst out laughing. "So let me get this right. You speak Khmai. You look Khmai. But you can't read this?"

Sophy smiled. "Right. Let me explain."

Twenty minutes later, Phearun said, "Wow, it must be strange for you, being Khmai but not feeling Khmai." Sophy shrugged her shoulders and gave no answer, as she was still figuring that out. Moving on, he said, "Let me tell you a bit about translation work. In order to be done well, it requires native speakers from both languages. You can find other translation places, but ours is the only one that always provides both. In fact, we have a whole team, British, American and Khmai. Teams of two work on each project initially, and then another team cross-checks. And there is another step: cultural translation. For example, some — actually, a lot of ideas do not make sense in the other culture, and new examples must be found." Phearun was getting carried away, and Sophy thought it was cool the way he seemed to love his work. As he was pacing, he stopped to turn towards her. "Do you know why we do this? Because the integrity of original documents is very important."

This time, Sophy was the one who laughed. "Where did you learn English? You use phrases like 'the integrity of original documents'!"

"Studying English is one thing. Translating is another level. I have improved a lot with this job." He smiled. "Miss Sophy, you are right. What you have here is a diary. Let me talk with my team and we will call you. It just so happens we are waiting on some cultural translation work. Which means we may have some open times in our schedule. But I cannot promise yet."

As Sophy was leaving, she noticed two small photo frames on Phearun's desk. "Is that your family?"

"Yes, this is my wife and my little boy and baby girl. And this one is from our wedding day," he beamed with pride and contentment.

Sophy looked closely at the wedding photo. It looked so much like her parents' wedding photo. A generation later, but the same traditional silk clothes. The difference was that Phearun and his bride were smiling. Sophy smiled back and turned to head for the doorway, but then paused and ran back in.

"Phearun . . . can you tell me the name? Her, or his name?"

Opening the older diary again to the first page, he read, "Kunthea. Her name is Gkun-tee-a." Looking up, he jumped into an explanation of Khmai names. "But it is most likely Sokunthea, Kunthea for short. A lot of Khmai names begin with 'So'. Somaly can be Maly, Socheatda can be Cheatda . . . and then there is Sovannara! That can be Vanna, Sovann, Nara, or Ra!" Sophy smiled at him, and he apologized. "Sorry, I get too excited. Names are one more aspect of language that I love."

"No worries! I think it is great that you love your work. Not everyone does."

On Monday afternoon, Sophy's cell phone rang. "Hello, is this Sophy Seng?"

The British accent was so strong it caught Sophy a bit off guard, and she paused before responding. "Yes . . . this is Sophy."

"This is Alistair Hill from Lighthouse. Phearun shared the project with us and we are keen to do it. But I hope you will understand, we are working around other projects, so we can only get it done in segments. Is that ok by you?"

"Yes, wonderful! Thank you so much!"

"Brilliant. I'll give you a shout when we have some of it done then."

Sophy was thrilled. For some reason she was feeling obsessed with the notebooks. She'd stared at the pages enough that images of the Khmai words were burned into her mind and she even dreamt about them. One thing she had noticed was that the letters had no spaces between words. It seemed the spaces were only between sentences with punctuation ending them. And there were question marks as well . . . the same as English. But what she had assumed were periods were different. What she really wanted to know was what the words said. Even in the short three weeks since she'd arrived, Cambodia was filling all her senses, and she had many questions.

CHAPTER SEVEN

The learning curve at Safe Space was high. It seemed that every expat worker was temporary, and the national Cambodian staff turned over a lot. Sophy tried to find a media policy in the digital files, but could not. "Just don't take photos of the girl's faces," Bethany had advised. So, she began the research to make a policy. She spent three days a week at the office in town and two days a week at the safe house in a village about thirty minutes' moto ride south. At the safe house, the girls, who had voluntarily joined the program, were learning marketable skills such as hairstyling or sewing. On Tuesdays and Thursdays, Sophy taught English classes. English could get them a position in the growing tourism industry, even if they did not have a high school diploma. Most of them had not been past third grade, but that was a matter of opportunity, not capacity to learn. Even in the first week, Sophy could tell which girls had the highest potential.

Sophy tried to steer clear of Bethany, but they inevitably clashed no matter what.

"What are you saying?" Bethany was perturbed.

"Uh, *gonlaing sovatapheap* . . . It means place of safety," Sophy explained, trying her best to not sound sarcastic. *Duh.* But as usual her face and tone gave her away. "Maybe you have not noticed, the Khmai staff have a hard time saying Safe Space, because Khmai does not have some of the sounds."

"So what? Now you are making fun of the language?" Pointing to the logo on the wall, which, curiously was written only in English, Bethany reminded Sophy, "We are called Safe Space . . . Say it right and they will learn to say it right."

Little by little, Sophy was piecing together realizations about the language, which leant understanding to her parents' difficulties with English. While it was clear that Khmai included certain sounds that did not even exist in English, the opposite was true as well. She'd given up on people being able to say the *fuh* sound in Sophy and just introduced herself as "So-pee". And while "s" was used at the beginning and the middle of words, it was never at the end. On this particular day, she was struck by the fact that none of the Khmai staff could say "Safe Space." It came out "Say-spay." This led to a secondary realization, that the organization was not named by the Khmai people, but by foreigners. And she wondered what other decisions they'd been left out of.

"Be careful, Miss Sophy," the house mom had warned her in Khmai. "Do not get too excited yet. These girls have hurting hearts. They need lots of counselling. They might lie to you." And then she said, "And also, you need to act more Khmai. You can speak ok, but they all know you are not Khmai. They expect that from the other interns, but you are Khmai blood."

Sophy was trying to learn to always bow with her hands pressed together, but it felt so weird. The only time she'd ever seen people do that was at a funeral her family attended in Ohio. Everyone there had been a Khmai refugee. Her parents tried to force her, and she'd balked.

CHAPTER EIGHT

Before closing the office at noon on Saturday, Phearun called. "Hello, Sophy, this is Phearun. We have eleven diary entries finished."

Sophy was thrilled. "Can you send it to me digitally?"

"No actually, I forgot to tell you. Until a piece is done and we know what the intended purpose is, it is still confidential. So we do not release it in a format that could be forwarded accidentally. We will print a copy for you to pick up here at Lighthouse, ok?"

"Sure, I understand that. When can I get it?"

"Well, it is all printed. I am leaving for home now. Can you meet me at Coffee Plus, the coffee shop at the Bokor Caltex gas station?"

Sophy knew the spot well. At the corner of Monivong and Mao Tse Toung streets, she had been stopping there on her way to the office for coffee. Although she'd heard that Starbucks was coming to Cambodia, they were not there yet. The little shop was right inside the mini-mart at the gas station, and they made decent lattes. If she got there early enough, she'd get a donut with her latte and buy a copy of the *Cambodia Daily*. Sophy liked the little daily paper. Unlike the Ohio papers, they did a great job of covering international news. There were very few ads and a small number of local news stories, which were not biased, she thought. Unlike TV, radio and Khmer papers, the English papers were still not censored.

"Sure! How soon can you be there?"

"Ten minutes!"

Sophy got there before Phearun, so she ordered a latte. She sat on the metal bar stool at the little window bar and watched the traffic coming in and going out of the gas station.

Two motos pulled up right outside her window and parked. Phearun pulled his white helmet off and pushed his fingers through his thick black hair, while stuffing his keys in his jeans pocket. He dismounted the bike, as the guy next to him took off his helmet and wiped the sweat from his brow. He was a tall white guy, with a tinge of red in his light brown hair. Hanging their helmets on their bike handle bars, they headed to the glass doors. Sophy caught Phearun's sight with a wave.

"Hi Sophy, this is Alistair Hill, my colleague at Lighthouse. We wanted to explain a few things about the translation."

Sophy shook his hand. "Nice to meet you. I believe we talked on the phone."

"Call me Ali." He had a big brother sort of smile and way about him, which made Sophy feel at ease. His eyes were pale green and kindly.

The three of them grabbed the only open table of the three. Squeezed between the coffee counter and a shelf full of crackers, it was a bit tight. The metal chairs screeched and clanked on the tile floor. Sophy had begun to realize that the tropics called for hard surfaces, like tile, metal and glass. Things like carpet and upholstery were quick to mold and hard to clean. She was still getting used to the general loudness of it all, cringing at the screeches.

Phearun pulled the translated papers from his backpack. They were stapled together on the left side and set into a blue plastic sleeve.

"I know I told you about some of the challenges of translation work already, but we wanted to tell you a bit more before you start reading," Phearun began.

Ali chimed in, "This diary is actually an amazing glimpse into Cambodian culture. It begins when Kunthea is only five years old. In fact she is too young to write in it herself, so her cousin is her scribe until she is eight." Sophy felt a strange excitement growing as they talked. The curiosity was killing her. "We wanted to ask you what you are thinking to do with the translation . . . not to give you a hard time. We just feel a great sense of gravity concerning the privacy of it," Ali continued as Sophy's mind worked to assimilate the word "privacy" with a short *i* sound.

"Well, I . . . I guess it makes sense to try and find her, if you think that is possible, and return it to her. What do you guys think?"

Phearun and Ali sighed in relief and smiled at each other and then at Sophy. "We'd say that is brilliant."

"We also think it is no accident that you found it and brought it to us. We are glad to be part of discovering the identity of Kunthea. Of course, we will need a lot more clues, but we suspect the future entries will give us the info we need." Ali paused and ran his fingers over the blue plastic document sleeve. "Sophy, we have looked ahead enough to know that this diary runs for a period of twenty-five years."

As the three of them sat in silence at the thought of that, Sophy thought about the fact that she was only three years old twenty-five years ago. And she wondered what her parents were like when she was only three. The shop had grown dark, as deep blue-grey rain clouds filled the sky. Small droplets on the window turned to torrents in a moment. A sea of motos flooded the gas station from every direction, seeking shelter beneath the huge metal overhang.

Phearun broke the quiet, "Also, we wanted to tell you that at times the translation may seem strange to you. For example, in these first twenty-four entries, Kunthea is age five to ten. We made a decision to translate some phrases in a literal way to keep the childlike way she talks as well as authenticity in the language. For example, when she talks about someone crying, she says 'They dropped their tears.'"

"Actually . . . that sounds beautiful." Sophy was caught off guard by the simple descriptive beauty of that phrase. She blinked back the tears forming in her own eyes. Embarrassed and surprised by her own emotions, she averted her eyes from Ali and Phearun, and sipped her latte.

Ali rescued her by moving on. "Lastly, although we have not done the translation work for the whole diary yet, we can see by thumb-ing through the entry dates that there may be entries missing. And some pages seem to have been ruined from water damage. So we can-not tell if she just did not write for a while — sometimes six months to two years later on in life — or if pages were actually lost. Nevertheless, we will be in touch when we have another set of entries done, at least a fortnight." Then seeing the confusion on Sophy's face, he clarified, "At least two weeks."

KUNTHEA'S DIARY PART ONE

April 10, 1987
Five years old

Where did this diary come from? My cousin gave it to me for Khmai New Year. She says I talk her ear off, so she got me this diary. For now I talk and she writes, but when I am bigger I will do the writing myself. My cousin is named Srey Srah. Her mama is Aunt Mony, and her papa is Uncle Heang. She is twelve, so she is good at writing. Before I tell you about today, my diary is pink and it has English letters on the cover. Srey Srah says the letters say "Happiness Memory". Oh, and my name is Kunthea and I am five years old!

Up on the road, they were dancing tonight. It is almost Khmai New Year. Mr. Vuen has a radio, so after the selling time tonight, they set it on the wooden selling table, and they danced in a circle around the table to the New Year music. Mr. Sok was dancing too hard and he fell on the table and broke it, but the radio was ok. Mr. Vuen cursed at Mr. Sok. Papa said that Mr. Sok drank up too much wine. Everybody went home after that.

It is so very hot! I do not want to sleep close to Sela and Sopheak because we make each other even more hot. So last night I moved out of the mosquito net and that was not as hot, but those mosquitos bit me all night long! I opened my tired eyes when the morning sun started to dance on my bamboo and leaf wall. The dried leaves on Mama's side of the hut cut the light up into little pieces that danced on my side. The dancing light woke me up. It has been a long time since I heard rain drops fall on my hut. When they do, it will be cool again I think.

I love the sound of our rain. Sometimes it starts with big drop-lets that *tap tap* at our soft hut. But soon it grows into a soft rumble that grows into a roaring flow that spills over the grass roof and to the ground where it makes little rivers in the dirt. Sometimes me and Sopheak, we lay on our tummies and peek through the bamboo floor slats and we watch the rivers grow. They dig into the red dirt and push and shove their way down the hill where they join up with the mighty Mekong. Sometimes there are rocks in the way. At first those rocks make the little rivers bend and then the power of the water bursts onto both sides, and suddenly those rocks become islands.

April 18, 1987
Five years old

Papa told me the story of a New Year angel. Her name is Mohurea Tevy. She likes to wear sparkly blue and green sapphires and she eats deer meat. She rides on a giant peacock and she carries a golden disc of power. All the New Year angels have the family name Tevy, because they had one father and he was the king of the gods. But a very smart rich boy was smarter than him and won a contest they had. It was a riddle contest, and the boy was so smart, he figured out the riddle. Since he won, the rich boy cut off the head of the god king! But the god king was so powerful that, if they threw his head in the ocean, it would all dry up! The god king had seven little girls and they are the New Year angels. Every year a different angel carries the head of the father around for that whole year because they cannot throw it in the ocean.

It sounds like an awful job. But Papa says the angels are happy . . . if we give them what they like. This one likes deer meat. I wonder where we will get deer meat. If I do not find deer meat, I'm afraid she might throw the golden power disc at me. I bet it would break my head instead of the other way around. Not like our plates. We only have six plates now because Sopheak dropped some. Now me and Sela, we eat off the same plate. I have never seen the ocean. Papa says it is like the Mekong but so big that you cannot see the other side! Anyway, Da says if the ocean dried up, the Mekong would too and we would have no fish to eat. So I am glad all the Tevy angels take turns carrying the head of the king around the world, even though that sounds terrible, and I am glad I do not have to.

August 4, 1987
Five years old

Our house stands up tall on four strong legs of wood. That is a good thing, because the Mekong is sneaky. It creeps up under our house fast. The houses on the road do not have legs. The road is high. But one time the Mekong creeped all the way up there also! They should sit on legs too, but they do not. Sotheary's house is up there. She has three brothers and she used to have a sister too, but the day the Mekong snuck up there, it took her sister away. The Mekong is powerful and dark in the rainy season. The monks came and chanted for three days, and the whole village thought that Sotheary's papa must have been awful bad in his life before, or *Preah Put* would not have let the Mekong take his little girl. After they stopped chanting, we could hear Sotheary's mama wailing and moaning all night long . . . even all the way from my house on legs down by the river.

Today, Mama grabbed the oiled tarp and spread it over our pile of nets and pillows, because the roof has more leaks than it did before. The tarp smells like the gasoline that the boy at the corner shop pours out of the giant Coke bottles and into Papa's moto. That shop is called the Lucky Lucky shop and they sell tasty little crackers fried in fish sauce, and moto gas from giant Coke bottles, but sometimes they are Marinda or Fanta bottles. I like that smell. When they pour it into Papa's moto, the smell puffs up in the air to my face. Then Papa pays the boy and swings me up onto my spot on the seat in front of him, and off we go!

September 10, 1987
Five years old

Da (Grandpa) and Yay (Grandma) live in the hut next door. It has legs, too. Today I was at their house when the sky grew dark. Then we all of a sudden heard the boats knocking each other, so I looked out to see the dark swirling river. In the rainy season, sometimes the Mekong looks angry, and in the dry season it looks almost dead. But there are some days when it just looks beautiful, strong and ringing with the happy music of the fishing boats and the swishing of their nets. On days like that, the blue sky and the sunlight join together and dance on the water! On days like that, I forget that the Mekong took Sotheary's sister away.

Then Da said, "The sky wants to rain, little one." Right then, while he was still saying that, the powerful wind slammed the shutters against the hut. I jumped back into Da's strong arms, which was a good thing because when the shutters slammed it was suddenly all dark and I could not even see! Then the rain hit Da's tin roof like tiny pebbles being poured all over it. Not like my roof. My roof is made of leaves and it is soft. So the rain sounds more like a swoosh than a crash. But soon even the loudness sounded smooth and steady. I tried to keep talking with Da, but he could not hear me over the loud rain on the roof. He smiled and shook his head no pointing at his ears. So, I fell asleep for a long time, and when the loud rain was over, the Mekong had climbed up the hill right to our houses! So, Da took an old fishing net and twisted it into a rope. He tied it to a piece of wood, set me on it and pushed me across the water to my own house! Mama cursed Da for that, but he did not hear it, which is a good thing since Da is Mama's papa, and she knows we have to respect our mamas and papas. She said I do not know how to swim yet, and that is the truth. I don't.

I love Da. Sometimes he makes me sad, and even scared. He has really bad dreams that make him yell out in his sleep. I can hear that from my own mat, under my own mosquito net, in my own house. Mama says his bad dreams are from the Pol Pot time. I do not know what the Pol Pot time is, because Mama gets upset when I ask about it. Her eyes get red and her face turns puffy, so I just feel strange, and I do not like to feel like that. But I really want to know. And my cousin, Srey Srah, who is writing this now for me, says her mama and papa also will not talk about the Pol Pot time. And she is also sad for Da. We both love him.

October 21, 1987
Five years old

There is dark power in the spirits. I know. Mr. Vuen has the spirits all the time. He is a weak man, so the powerful spirits just walk right into his body whenever they want to. Sopheak and I can hear the voices screaming. The voices change, but they all come from his own mouth! I saw that. We don't want to look . . . but then we do want to. We agreed we should not get too close, or the spirits may try to just walk right into us too. Sopheak and me, we think that little children are not as strong as grown-ups, so that could happen. We are not strong enough to hold the rope on Uncle Heang's boat when the Mekong is fighting with it. And we are not strong enough to carry Mama's food basket from the market the whole way. We have to stop and rest, but Mama can walk the whole way.

One time I did look at Mr. Vuen when the spirits had him. I peeked through the window bars and there he was, with his sons holding him down on the wooden bed stand. One on each leg and one on each arm, the sons were sweating and making faces. His shirt was all torn and his pants too. His eyes were rolling back in his head. When I saw that, I turned to run away, but my hands got caught in the window bars and I cried out. Then he looked right at me with his spirit eyes! Now that spirit knows what I look like, so I make Mama braid my hair everyday now so I look different and maybe the spirit cannot find me. I can't tell Mama why, that the spirit saw me. So I just tell her it is my new style, and she smiles in my face and tilts her head and says, "Oh, my little Kunthea." Mama's hair is blackest black and silky smooth. It hangs down longer than her shoulders. Usually she wears it up in a bun, but I love it most when she has just washed it at the bien. She rubs out the extra water with a krama and combs it out as she leans to each side. The morning sun dances on it and makes it dry fast. But as it dries, it begins to curl and toss all around her beautiful smiling face. When she goes to a wedding she puts on makeup and that is pretty, but not as pretty as her face when the morning sun comes up over the hill and dances on her freshly washed hair at the bien.

November 12, 1987
Five years old

Papa says that he will teach me to swim next year (when I am six) in March, right before the Khmai New Year, because the Mekong loses some of its power then since it has not rained in a long time and it will not take me away like Sotheary's sister. Sotheary's grandma says that the sister is walking around in the next life with wet clothes on forever, cold and sick and hungry, because the Mekong took her before she had her dinner that day and she still had on her school clothes. So sometimes I dream that I see a little girl on the muddy slope by Da's house. Just standing there. Her blue pleated skirt is streaked with mud, and her white shirt is not white. She even has her Hello Kitty school bag. I can see the little bright pink kitty face through the smeared mud. The zipper is torn and her school writing book is hanging out. The one with the picture of Angkor Wat. But I will never tell Sotheary about that dream. They have many spirit houses and shrines at their house. More than us. Sotheary's sister's spirit lives in one of them, and they try to feed her all the time. They put bananas and rice there every day. One time I saw a can of Coke there, too! Everybody knows that Coke costs a lot of money. The birds and the dogs and ants eat the offerings, but her sister gets strength from it when they light the tall incense sticks right in front of it. One time me and Sotheary sat and watched the thin little ribbons of smoke twirling up in the air, and I tried to see the offering food floating up inside the smoke, but I could not. If they do not do this, the sister will give them many problems. Even worse than being hungry. She already makes Sotheary's mama have terrible dreams. No one knows her name anymore . . . They must not, because they never say it.

March 2, 1988
Six years old

Papa almost forgot that today is March 1. He promised me he'd teach me to swim in March. But he finally got home at 4:30 and we still had one-and-a-half hours before dark. When I heard Papa's moto coming, I ran up the ladder and put on my stretchy shorts and t-shirt. Papa's moto needs a new sound softener part, as it is really loud. Papa jumped off his moto and said, "Is there a little girl here who wants to learn to swim?" I jumped up and down saying, "Me, me!" He did not forget. He ran up the ladder to change out of his police clothes and I waited and it seemed like a long time, probably because I was so excited. In his undershirt and shorts, he swooped me up and ran to the river bank with me in his big strong arms, and the jiggling made me laugh. The river bank is dry and crusty now since we have had no rain for five months, so I shielded my face from the dusty wind. With both hands on my shoulders, he squatted in front of me, looked me in the eyes and said, "Are you sure you want to learn to swim, *goan*, little one?" I laughed at him, because Papa *knows* I want to learn to swim! He was teasing me. He stepped onto the half-rotten wood planks that lead out to the fishermen's docks. When we got out far enough, he turned around, his back to the water, and made a very serious face at me. Then he just fell backwards into the water! As my mouth hung open in surprise, he disappeared under the brown water and soon popped right back up!

I screamed, "How do you float like that Papa? Just like the dead fishes!"

"Ah, that is my secret. But do not worry — I am not dead! Ok, now you jump in!"

And I did. I did not even stop to think about that, because Papa was already there, and how could I be safer than with my Papa?

I held onto Papa's big shoulders and he showed me how to work my arms, kick my feet and even how to make my hands to be like the fins on the fish. And I learned to swim! But Papa says I still need practice. He says to do anything good, we have to practice it a lot. But I still wonder how the fish swim better than us when they have no feet to kick with.

June 5, 1988
Six years old

Papa has a moto, and then we have one bicycle for our family. Papa taught me and Sopheak to ride the bike this year. Usually I do not sit on the seat because my feet do not reach the pedals. But Sopheak, he has a fancy way of sitting on the seat and pushing the pedals down each time they come back up; he pushes them so hard that they come back up and he catches them with his feet again. Right then left. Push, catch, push, catch. He is only four, almost five, and I am already six, so tomorrow I will learn to do this too. When I keep my feet on the pedals, in a standing position, I have to arch my back to keep it from scraping on the seat, but sometimes it still bumps, and that hurts. Mama let me ride to the market to buy a banana flower yesterday. So when I ate that banana flower in my dinner salad, it tasted the best ever, because I went to the market myself and bought it. But riding the moto with Papa is better. He sets me down safely between his legs on the seat and even when there is no wind at all, we make wind! At first it makes me laugh and then, after a bit, it makes me sleepy. Last time we went to Papa's oam's house, I fell asleep hard. I could feel Papa's strong arm close around me and catch me before I could fall.

Oam Seng lives four villages away, so it takes us a long time to get there. Mama does not like Oam Seng so she will not go. I asked her why and she just says she is too busy to go, but me and Sopheak, we think she does not like Oam Seng, or maybe his wife. Mama says that his wife took him away from his first family. I even saw her roll her eyes at Papa when he made a joke about that. Mama did not think it was funny, so Papa just quickly closed his mouth and set me on the moto and off we went. I played with Uncle Seng's little girl while he and Papa talked about the prime ministry. Papa always whispers when he talks about the prime ministry, and sometimes he looks around to make sure no one is looking. Then I also look around to see who might be listening. Papa said the prime ministry pays his wages, so he has to follow them. Then Oam Seng says he can just pretend to follow and that is ok. I am not sure where the prime ministry is going and why we should follow. Anyway, his wife is always nice to us and she gives us candy treats! And his little girl, she is like my cousin far off. She is so cute. She is only three years old, not big like me. Her mama loves having me around to help play with my cousin, while she watches the television. So, it is a happy time to go there.

July 15, 1988
Six years old

Today the giant puppet people were out on parade to get money for the monks since it is the beginning of rainy season. Mama says that for these two months every year, the monks are not allowed to come out and get it themselves like usual. The puppet people always try to make us kids laugh, but we are so afraid. Who wouldn't be? They are like two papas tall and have scary painted smile faces on giant hard shiny heads, that never change, like they are stuck that way. And that is scary. Because nobody is happy all the time.

First comes the way-too-slow moto music cart, screeching out the jumpy music and the booming voices that call us out to pay. Then behind them is the giant puppet people, dancing around and swinging their big hard heads to look right at us kids! As the music motos rumble down the street to scare more kids, next come the old folks with their tin dishes to collect money for the monks: old men in baggy white tunics that hang off their skinny bodies, and ladies in their funeral clothes. I wonder why they tell us to be happy and then they wear funeral clothes. Last time, all the grown-ups tried to make me go put the money in. "Look how *fun*!" But I can't stand getting so close to the puppet people. I just ran up the ladder and stuffed my face in the bunched-up mosquito netting in the corner. I tried pulling it around my whole head and pressing it against my ears, but the sound still crawled right into my ears.

So after a while Mama or Papa did it themselves, because we have to pay. They bowed and dropped some riel in the tins, and laughed, "*Goan knyom ian*. My child is just shy." I wonder why grown-ups think the fake giant puppet people are fun. Don't they remember being scared?

September 22, 1988
Six years old

I have been six for a whole nine months now. I know because I was born in January and now it is the middle of rainy season and the river is high. So, when we have floods, I know I am getting closer to being a whole year older. Last night, the Mekong snuck up under our houses while we slept.

I saw Uncle Heang trying to get up the ladder of his house today and he fell into the Mekong below! Papa saw it too, and he grabbed Uncle Heang with his big strong arms and pulled him back to the ladder. They both held on to the ladder and rested their heads on it, breathing hard, while their legs floated with the Mekong. But Uncle Heang only has one leg. Nobody talks about how he got that way. He is Papa's brother.

Uncle Heang and Aunt Mony live in a concrete house next to ours. The upstairs is wood, and every year they have to live all upstairs because of the Mekong moving in and out of the downstairs. Srey Srah is their daughter who gave me this diary.

October 17, 1988
Six years old

Aunt Mony was screaming today. When we got to her house, she was jumping around and shaking her hands about with big fish eyes!

"Jump back! It's a snake!" It was the kind that looks like the Naga except with one head, not seven. A Cobra. A boy I know from school, his brother was bit by a cobra. He got fever and then his leg started falling apart until he died.

Mr. Vuen and Mr. Sok came running with bamboo poles and big threshing knives. We stayed outside the house.

"*Now, now!*" There was a big thud and more screams, and then slashing sounds. Aunt Mony appeared in her doorway, with a sick look on her face, and then suddenly fell face down!

I screamed, "Aunt Mony is dead! She was bit by a snake!" I did not want to see her legs fall off, so I ran to Mama and stuffed my face in her tummy and I could not even breathe.

Then Sopheak grabbed my arm. "Kunthea! She is not dead. She fainted." Mrs. Sok had rolled Aunt Mony over by then and was shaking her. I could see her breathing and coughing so I knew Sopheak was right. She was not dead.

Then Mr. Vuen came out of the house, laughing, with the bloody snake hanging limp from his bamboo pole. When I knew for sure it was dead, I went and looked at it. Samrith told me that snakes have green blood. But that is not true. It is red just like us.

When Uncle Heang got home, he and Aunt Mony had a fight about whether they should cook the snake in soup or sell it. By the time they agreed to sell it, it was covered in red tree ants, so they just threw it all in the hot oil together and cooked it up. So we all had deep fried snake and red ants with our rice, and we gave some to Mr. Sok and Mr. Vuen's families too. Really, the snake was two meters long when we stretched him out, so there was plenty for everyone!

CHAPTER NINE

Sophy

Sophy groggily grabbed for her ringing phone on the rattan bedside table. Her lamp was still on. She had fallen asleep shortly after finishing, while reflecting on what she had read. She squinted at the screen: 9:20 a.m., July 10, 2016. Because of plans she'd made with friends from Safe Space, Sophy was only able to read a few entries before heading out for the evening the night before. There was a live band at the Foreign Correspondence Club, known as the FCC. Best known for stories on war correspondents who hung out there during the Vietnam War and events leading up to the Khmai Rouge genocide, the building itself was historic. Some of the scenes in the famous 1980s' film, "The Killing Fields," were filmed at the FCC.

Set on a corner right on the riverfront, a huge wooden staircase led from the ground floor to the first floor, where there were rooms for rent. Another set of stairs leading to the restaurant and bar were so narrow that people waited at the bottom while others descended, and vice versa. Like many stairways of the French colonial era, they were curvy white terrazzo. On a busy night, that narrow stairway seemed to spill people into the spacious open-air room like wine from a bottle. Heavy black ceiling fans hung from massive wood beams under a terra-cotta tile roof. The underside of the terra-cotta roof revealed a huge lattice of soldered black metal, each little tile hanging by its hooked edge. The whole tile structure was held there by sheer gravity and yet they provided solid protection from the monsoon rains. One long terrazzo bar curved along the outside edge, providing patrons a view of the Tonle Sap River and the nightlife below. Several sets of four sturdy wood chairs with deep red leather cushions surrounded low-set round wooden tables. The solid wood bar encircled a huge all-brick wood-fired oven. Sophy found herself at a table with several NGO workers and international school teachers. It was happy hour, and the noise level increased as the alcohol flowed.

"To the French!" Thomas toasted. "For leaving Cambodia with baguettes, cheese and beautiful buildings like this!"

Sophy sipped on a glass of red wine and tried to stay engaged, but her mind kept drifting back to Kunthea and her diary. So, when no one was looking, she slipped away down the terrazzo stairs and looked for a tuk-tuk ride home.

Sret had warned Sophy about the tuk-tuk drivers who sought business at these touristy spots. "Check the floor of the tuk-tuk. Do you see beer cans? Look at their eyes. Are they red?" Sophy was already seeing how her language ability, albeit limited, was a huge benefit. The first guy who called to her motioned to his tuk-tuk, as if it was a done deal. Leaning in enough to see, she saw there were five empty beer cans on the floor. "*Neac Na puck nih dteang ah*? Who drank all of these? I do not want to ride with a drunk tuk-tuk driver!" The other drivers who had gathered to hear the negotiation burst out laughing, and another one who seemed sober offered her a ride at a fair price.

Back at her apartment, she settled into her bed, and started to read again by midnight. She remembered finishing the entries and then lay there awake, her head swimming with thoughts of spirit houses and temple roofs and weddings. Images of her parents' wedding photos floated about in her mind, and she wondered if they had loved each other or just learned to over the years.

"Sophy . . . Sophy! Were you asleep? Sophy, there was a shooting." It was Jessica, another intern at Safe Space. Her voice trembled, "Right at the Bokor Caltex coffee shop!"

CHAPTER TEN

Sophy sat up on the edge of her bed, rubbing the back of her neck and wondering if she was dreaming. "What are you talking about? Who? I was just there yesterday!" Sophy could hear yelling in Khmai, and wailing, in the background over the phone.

Jessica stammered, "I am here now. I was stopping by for a coffee. I had parked my moto and was taking off my helmet . . . when I heard loud sounds . . . shots . . . three I think, and then screaming . . ." Her voice shook and she broke down crying. "Can I come over? I am . . . so scared."

Ten minutes later, Jessica was at the gate. Sophy ran down the stairs in her PJs and bare feet to tell the guard it was ok to let her in. Back in her apartment, Sophy flipped open her MacBook, and they got on Jessica's Facebook page. The posts were popping up every second. Photos and videos of the scene taken by onlookers were streaming in. One of them showed, through the front window, a pregnant woman kneeling over the body of a man who lay in a pool of blood. He was lying on the floor right by the table where she had sat with Phearun and Ali less than twenty-four hours before; she knew from the mini-mart shelving behind the table, the one with the crackers. She felt sick.

Who is this man? she was wondering when newscasts started popping up. It was Kem Ley, a well-known political analyst who had been recently quoted in the *Cambodia Daily* the day before. He had commented on a report that had exposed the extreme (and probably ill-gotten) wealth of a top official's family. Soon, messages were flooding Sophy's phone. A few were from colleagues who had begun to hear the news, but mostly, they were from her parents. She wondered how it could be that her parents were so clueless most of the time, and then an event like this happens in Cambodia, half a world away, and they know immediately.

Her American sense of justice was rocked by the fact that they were watching the aftermath of a murder live, on Facebook, right down the street from where it happened, in broad daylight in a very public setting. In fact, it was an assassination.

In preparing for her internship, she had read about politically motivated assassinations of the early 2000s, but that was so long ago. Surely the country had moved forward, realizing that the world is now too global and they are being watched over the Internet. Technology was providing international accountability like never before. Surely they knew that blatant assassination of activists and opponents would get them nowhere in the modern world. It was just so . . . primitive.

Jessica asked if she could move into Sophy's place after this. She was only twenty-two and had not ever lived alone. The current events had given them both a reality check. There were two bedrooms anyway. But Sophy hid the diary papers in her dresser.

None of the expat workers felt like going out to bars after the shooting of Kem Ley, at least for a couple weeks. So, they hung out at their own places, and their conversations leaned towards more significant topics. In some ways, they were all cut from similar cloth. Idealists. Dreamers. Adventurers. Activists. Self-proclaimed heroes. In Cambodia short-term, none of them had studied the Khmai language, other than a few simple practical phrases. At times it seemed they had to study each other's English, since they used different terms. Sophy was catching on and expanding her own vocabulary.

"Toss this in the rubbish bin," or the trash can.

"Where is the water closet?" She'd had an ah-ha moment when she connected this with bathroom doors marked "WC".

"That place is dodgy," which meant it was shady or questionable.

So far she had been hanging out most with Matthias, Thomas (his neighbor who taught history at an international school) and Jessica.

Matthias was a thoughtful guy. But he was young, right out of undergrad school. His Swiss accent, and even the way he phrased his English, lent a certain charm to his curiosity. And he had that European look and demeaner that Sophy found quite attractive. His blonde hair tousled from a loosely defined partition on the right side. The slight weight of the hair seemed to cause a continual slight tilt of his head to the left. His eyes were pale green with a hint of blue, like a certain tone of the green sapphires she'd seen in the market. His jawline was sharp with a well-defined nose, the kind of nose the Khmai would rant about: "Oh, so beautiful! It has structure. Not flat with no bones, like ours."

Jessica turned out to be a good roommate. She was introverted enough to enjoy her time alone, which suited Sophy fine. She had wavy long blonde hair, which had gone from wavy to outright curly with the Cambodian humidity. She wore no makeup, because she didn't need to. With pale blue eyes, freckles and a Greek goddess nose, she attracted more attention than she wanted in Cambodia. And after a few weeks of the heat, she had her golden locks cut to shoulder length.

Bethany, so far, had kept her distance. She clearly had hopes of working long term in non-profit work. It seemed as though that had been her plan a long time, but Sophy could not tell if Safe Space and Cambodia were just a stepping stone towards bigger things. She had shoulder-length light-brown hair, the tips of which were dyed purple. She spent most of her time outside of work writing a blog about the hardships of expat life in Cambodia.

So far Sophy had managed to make Bethany laugh exactly once, when she was teaching Sophy to ride the loaner Honda Chaly *moto*, a moped bike she had from Safe Space. Sophy didn't quite get the subtle part of the handlebar throttle. She zoomed across the courtyard and crashed into a potted plant that promptly fell over. Seeing the previously deceased plant on the ground, encompassed by dry dirt and broken clay, she'd exclaimed, "Look, I killed it!"

It was one such Friday evening when Sophy's phone rang. Seeing Phearun's name on her screen, she hurried into another room so her friends would not hear her conversation and ask unwanted questions.

"Sophy, sorry I didn't call earlier today. We were super busy at Lighthouse. But I have the next set, fourteen entries. We are open half-days on Saturday if you want to stop by."

KUNTHEA'S DIARY PART TWO

October 28, 1988
Six years old

After dinner tonight, Mama lit the candle and sat at the table. She pulled all the papers out of her teacher bag and began to mark them with her pen. Mama is a teacher. She is smart and kind and patient and she loves her students. I am so lucky that she is my mama, because she taught me most my letters before I even went to school. She never really got to study a lot, but after the Pol Pot time, they needed teachers and Mama was so smart they let her become a teacher. Mama told me that no one went to school in the Pol Pot time, because the red Khmai soldiers wanted all of them to be farmers. I asked why they were called the red soldiers, but she just started talking about something else. She does that sometimes. Anyway, all the kids in my village, they know my mama like she is famous. And she taught all of them their letters in school, so they love her and call her "necru" (teacher). It makes me so proud, a feeling like my chest is full of happy air, when I hear the other kids call my mama *Necru*. I wonder if the red Khmai were red because they spent too much time running around in the red dirt.

November 7, 1988
Six years old

We heard some yelling and screaming tonight, so Papa went to see about it. He is a police man. We were already under our nets and Papa was only wearing his *krama*. By the time I heard the crying in the distance, I could see through my net. In the moonlight, Papa was pulling on his pants and doing the button as he scurried for the ladder.

"It's ok. Papa will be back soon. It is not far," Mama whispered.

Most policemen take money from people when they settle their fights, but not Papa. He just tries to help people. He gets his money from the government once a month and gives it to Mama. There is one wooden table in our house, for everything: for folding clothes and counting money, and cleaning the rice, and writing our schoolwork. In the rainy season, we even pluck chickens there, because the ground below sometimes fills up with the Mekong. There is one drawer in the table, and it has a lock. Mama locks the money in there and then she hides the key in a little secret pocket in her bra, under her bosoms. That pocket has a zipper so she will never lose the key. That is a secret. And I told my cousin not to tell and she said, "It's ok. My mama has a secret zipper pocket in her bra too." And my cousin said they sell those bras at Orussey Market in the city.

December 13, 1988
Six years old

Last night I could not go to sleep, so I lay there just listening to Da and Papa talking. Da can speak the *barang* (French) language, but he does not do it because he hates the *barang*. A long time ago, before Da was born, his own papa worked at a *barang* palace on a mountain called the Cows Hump. I do not know why they called it the Cows Hump, but they just did. It was high on a mountain. Da's papa was a cook there. Da said that all the *barang* came there to have big fancy parties and get drunk and play betting games. They let some rich Khmai come there too. Da told Papa that the *barang* treated his papa like cow poop. Now

Da's papa was poor, and everybody knows that poor people got that way because of the bad stuff they did in the life when they lived before they died and then came back. So rich people treat poor people like cow poop. They think they deserve it. But Da said it is not right. He gets angry when he talks about that. I heard some of that story before. But this time there was something new. Da told Papa that over one thousand poor Khmai people died when they were building that palace and the long road going up the mountain to get there. They made them work all day and night with no food. And some of them just fell right off the mountain. They must have hit their heads on the rocks at the bottom of the mountain and that made them die. The *barang* had lots of power. That was back in the olden days when they were in charge of Cambodia.

January 8, 1989
Seven years old

"You know, if your sister died, when she came back she would not be your sister. She'd be someone else or an animal if she was bad." I had a fight with Sotheary about that. "That is not true! When people die they come back!" And then Sotheary's big eyes filled up with tears, and I remembered. Her sister never came back. Sotheary's aunt Tata pulled her close. "Little ones, reincarnation means your soul comes back as someone else. It is the cycle of life."

"I know, but then why is Mama still looking for my sister? And why do we feed her ghost?" Sotheary sniffled.

"Because we never know for sure. We can't know."

February 16, 1989
Seven years old

AaahhGaa-ai-da-mi-ah-aaahhh baaa-ba-ba . . .

I sat right up and got my face tangled in the mosquito net. Somebody died. The monk's chants have no singing, just words, but not even words, just sounds. I think it sounds ugly but I will not say so, because it is the monks. Papa was climbing down the ladder, so I followed him. Sela and Sokaa are too little, so they stayed with Mama and the twins, but Sopheak came with me. We are five and seven now, much braver than the little ones. We held hands tightly and watched Papa walk towards the sound. It was down by the river. It was still dark but the moon was bright, so me and Sopheak, we snuck down towards the river. Then the moon was hiding behind a cloud, so there was not much light. I gripped Sopheak's arm tight as we crept up closer, when suddenly we saw him! It was my friend Vannara's da. He looked like he was sleeping on that table, but we knew from the chanting he was dead. Dead bodies make me feel strange, because I know they are empty. The spirit has left and you never really know if it is angry or sad and what to do about all these things.

So I just looked at Vannara's da's old body and thought that maybe it was hollow inside since the spirit is gone. And then I got a chill thinking that spirit could be hanging over us right then! Sopheak must have thought so too, because he grabbed my arm and we both started to run back home, but we slipped on the dry crumbly dirt. My heart was pounding so hard that I didn't even care about scraping my knee. We scrambled up the ladder of our own hut, and Mama tried to scold us. But we could not hear her; the chanting was way too loud. We just saw her mouth moving and finger pointing with a mad look on her face. When I lay back on my mat, I wondered about what Aunt Tata said. We can never know . .... if dead people are in someone else or a rat in the fish market.

Papa said they do not know why he died. Maybe it was high blood. But Vannara's mama and papa were so afraid of his spirit and all the spirits, they got the monks to stay and yell chants in the microphones for three whole days. It was terrible. No sleeping for us.

We watched the twins and Sokaa and Sela when Mama and Papa and Yay and Da went to the funeral. Mama has one brown and black wrap skirt for funerals. She wears it with a plain white top with buttons in front. I saw her use her secret key to open the drawer. She took out some money to take there. Mama said we needed to give that money so Vannara's mama and papa could pay for the monks to chant and all the incense and food for the guests. Papa said it is more important to protect our village from evil spirits, so after that we only had rice and nothing else for dinner for two days. I think Papa is right, because evil spirits make people sick and die and all sorts of bad stuff. And anyway, rice fills me up. It just does not taste so good all by itself.

March 1, 1989
Seven years old

Mama says that *Preah Put* (Buddha) wants us to be good. If we do not, then we have to give more offerings to the Preah Put statues at the temple, and to the monks. There are other god statues at the temple also. I think Mama is very worried about it because she takes us to the temple a lot. We put rice and little pots of incense in front of lots of different gods there. I do not know why Mama is so worried, because I think she is good. Mama even keeps extra incense in the special drawer of the wooden table, in case we need it after the market closes at night.

March 22, 1989
Seven years old

This morning, the sun was dancing on the temple roofs, so they glittered like gold! I sat on the top stair of our hut ladder and squinted my eyes at the bright dancing golden light, while the breeze puffed up my hair. Then Mama called out, "Kunthea! Your chores!"

I am seven now so I have important chores.

"Get the comb so I can do your hair or the dirt will put it all in knots."

I finished sweeping under the house just in time for noodle breakfast. Yay makes the best *gootee-ew (noodle soup)* in our village. That's what I think. She gets up at 5:00 a.m. and boils a huge pot of water and puts a kilo of oxtail in it to make the broth. Then she adds lots of fancy spices. Sometimes she lets me grind the spices in the stone grinder bowl. Then she adds the rice noodles, and they turn clear colored when they are cooked. And then she puts in the chopped pork. She said that rich people use beef, but pork is good enough for us. Before we eat it, we squeeze a lime over it and sprinkle crispy bean sprouts on top. So tasty!

One time I was in a city market with Aunt Mony, and I saw little glass jars of teeny tiny bits of real gold! My eyes bugged right out of my head, and Aunt Mony said it was not real; they just mix it with some smelly liquid and make gold paint for the temples. There are many monks at the temple . . . and little boys my own age that are trying to be monks, too. They study the words of Preah Put (Buddha). And all of them, big and small, wear the saffron orange sheet robes. Most of them do not wear sandals. I did not tell anyone this . . . but I saw a monk smoking a cigarette one time. They are not supposed to do that. So, I just pray to Preah Put because I think that monk will have a really bad next life or might be a rat. I guess he deserves it, but it seems wrong to me that his whole next life would be bad just because he did one bad thing in this life. I just pray and do not think about it. No one can know that I think that. I just do, but I never say it out loud, in case Preah Put or the other gods can hear me. And I made cousin swear not to tell ("Make sure you write that," Kunthea says, and I do J).

May 5, 1989
Seven years old

Sopheak and I played on the fishing boats today. Uncle Heang has his own boat. Papa let him take me and Sopheak on the boat into the Mekong before the sun came up! We were like a little island that moved through the water without getting wet. The wind blew my hair back from my face, and I closed my eyes and smiled because that felt so nice. Me and Sopheak, we laughed when we saw the dark people from our village moving away from us and getting smaller, like lizards and then ants.

Uncle Heang threw his big net into the Mekong. He half leans on the long oar that is attached to the boat and uses his one leg to make him steady and strong. I saw his muscles bumping around in his arms as he lifted the net high above his head. At first slow, and then fast, he circled the bunched-up net over his head, one, two, three, four times. Then on the fourth time, he let go of all but one string, and we just watched while the net floated on the air, and then down, down, down it floated and set on the water with a soft swoosh. I felt like I was floating on the air, too, while I watched it. Then it started to sink under the water. Uncle Heang was in the front, then Sopheak and then me. Sopheak tried to do everything Uncle Heang did, but with a pretend net. That was kind of cute and I smiled, but Sopheak did not see me. Then we just waited a long while. The sun was up and it felt hot on my skin, and I wished we could fly through the Mekong again, but we had to wait on the fish. Then finally, I saw it! The strings in his hands started pulling like they were alive! Then me and Sopheak, we helped him pull the net into the boat. We both fell back onto our bottoms and suddenly the fish were jumping around us in the net. "Wow, they are so wiggly! Not like the ones in the market."

"Those ones are worn out, little ones," Uncle Heang explained. "They are the same fish. Just tired from all the flopping they do in the boat."

June 28, 1989
Seven years old

It is June now, and the *mien* fruit is so heavy! In our village there are five mien trees. The first one is at the corner near Sotheary's house. The second one is down by Vannara's house. The third one is at the ice seller's house near the market. And the last two are right near the main big road, before you get to the Lucky Lucky Shop. All five of the trees look like they are crying now, and people are propping up their heavy branches with bamboo poles. It is because the mien fruit is big and juicy. That is what makes the branches so heavy and drooping.

"We should just eat the *mien* fruit and then they would not have to prop them up like that." Sopheak is always looking for a reason to eat.

"No, silly, the fruits are not ready yet! Do you want your *mien* sweet or not?" I explained how it works to him, because I am older and I know. At least they are not so brown and dusty now, since the rains have finally come. Won't be long now, and we will eat all the *mien* we want!

January 6, 1990
Eight years old

Today is the day I start writing in my diary by myself. Srey Srah is fifteen now and she had to go work in a factory, so she does not have time to listen to me talk and do all the writing. She says I need to practice my writing anyway.

I am eight now, and the cold season is here. Sela sleeps with me. She is five. Sopheak is six and Sokaa sleeps with him. Sokaa is only three. And Malia and Mony are just one year old, so they sleep between Mama and Papa. Sometimes they still wake up at night, especially Malia. But with Mama right there, they can nurse, and in no time our house is quiet again. Mama softly laughs and whispers to Papa, "Two short suckles and she is fast asleep again." Our nets are full of us each night. In the cold season, that keeps us warm.

But Papa missed dinner last night. He did not come home until after bedtime. But I was not asleep and I heard Mama talking to him under the house. She told him to take a bath at the *bien* (water pot), in an angry but still quiet voice. But he just came right up the ladder and fell onto his mat. He talked funny and he fell onto his mat instead of just lying down. Mama was right. Papa needed a bath. He smelled bad. Maybe Papa thought it was too cold for a bath. Then I did not feel safe, so I could not fall asleep for a long time. But I scooted closer to Sela to stay warm. Mama must have stayed under the house for a long time, because I fell asleep before she came upstairs.

February 11, 1990
Eight years old

Sotheary's older cousin is getting married! They had the *Pjo-ap Piak* (sticking word/promise ceremony) to make the engagement promise. It is almost as fancy as the wedding! They both wore beautiful lime-green traditional silk clothes. I saw the clothes hanging on the metal hanger in the house before they got dressed. Her top had so many jewels on it that I could not count them. I tried three times but kept losing track. They were pink like lotus, and white like jasmine, and orange like the monk's robes. I decided that someday I would learn to sew those clothes and maybe work at Mr. Hong's shop. The girls there sew on the jewels with tiny needles and long threads, all day long. I wonder if they get to choose the colors or Mr. Hong does? The wedding will be in May, after Khmai New year and just before it rains.

May 3, 1990
Eight years old

Me and Sela and Sotheary, we got up at 3:00 a.m.! She spent the night on our mat because her house was too full of relatives from the provinces. We scurried along the road giggling and scaring the night rats away. The moonlight cast our shadows on the dirt so the rats thought there were lots of us! Ha! Not just three. We got to her cousin's house, kicked off our flip flops, climbed the ladder and there she was — the bride! The one hanging light bulb was burning dim, but there was an extra one set up to a car battery too. She sat quietly on the mat, her legs tucked under her in the proper way a grown-up girl sits. She was getting married, so she had to practice that I think. The hairdresser lady was there with all her stuff: baskets of pins and combs, and silk flowers and hair spray. We snuck over to her box when she was not looking and stirred up the pins with our fingers. Sela picked up a clear rubber band, the kind you cannot even see, and just then the hair lady saw us and she smacked Sela's hand. So, we all moved back against the wooden wall. Then the hair lady was teasing her hair with a comb, but it was not working. She made a face and tried again, pulling hard and making the bride frown. After a long while she attached a big extra chunk of fake hair on the back of her head and combed the real hair over it. Another lady was working on her nails: beautiful bright pink with tiny diamonds on each end! Sotheary's aunt Tata said they were not real diamonds, but I do not believe it. Then they did her makeup. First, they made her face all powdery and whiter, even her lips and eyebrows. That was kind of scary looking. But then they added all kinds of paint and fake eyelashes. I looked over at Sela while the makeup lady was drawing the bride's lips on with a red pencil. She had her own little head tilted back and her lips pushed out. Sela is so cute sometimes.

After a long time, Sotheary's cousin looked perfect, just like Mama in the wedding photo on the wall in my hut. Then Sotheary's yay brought the bride some bawbaw (rice soup). She was so hungry for that soup, but the makeup lady yelled at her to not mess up her makeup. I saw an old *krama* scarf on the stair railing, and I gave it to the bride. She did not say anything, but she did smile at me while she spread it across her front so she could eat the bawbaw. I knew she wanted me to keep the secret we had together and not tell the hair lady she was eating. I kept watch at the door in case she came. Sela and Sotheary just watched me do all of this, because they are shyer than me. Well, Sela is not really shy, just around grown-ups is all.

At 5:00 a.m., they brought the pig hind legs on platters to add to the fruit and cake gifts that were set out the night before. The wooden beds under the house were all completely covered with silver bowls full of fruit and wrapped desserts. All the grown-ups ran around telling people what to do. There was a morning breeze that made the wedding tent puff up and then drift back down. And I started to feel sleepy just watching it. Poof up, float down, poof up, float down. I was dozing off and starting to have a dream when suddenly the music started. It was so loud I jumped and fell off my blue plastic chair. Then I knew it must be 6:00 a.m., when the music starts. I had watched the wedding set-up men put the speaker up yesterday. They tied it to a coconut tree with some strong rope. The big silver horn stood way up in the sky like that coconut tree that had something to say, and I had to hold my ears when they tested it.

People came in and out of the tent and the house all day. Me and Sela and Sotheary snuck around the back and watched the cooks. The chicken man had a huge cleaver knife. First, he whacked off the heads. Then he whacked the whole chicken a bunch more times and threw all the pieces in the giant tin bowl: feet, intestines, wings, legs all mixed together. The pig lady carried the pig head by its ear and threw it in a cooler bin. But she did not close the lid, so we went up to look, and the pig head was smiling at me! Vannara and some other boys were hiding in the tent curtains, waiting for people to finish their beers and Cokes so they could get the cans and take them to the recycle shop and get money. Sotheary's mama wanted us to watch for kids who were hiding there to steal the gift money envelopes, but we knew they just wanted the cans. The bride and groom changed their jeweled outfits five times through the day. Pink, then yellow, then purple, then green and finally white at the end. My favorite were the pink ones. And they wore the pointy shoes like the New Year's Angels! I am not going to tell anybody, but Sotheary's cousin did not look happy to me. Sotheary said she did not really love her new husband. Mama told me that brides and grooms learn to love each other after the wedding.

September 23, 1990
Eight years old

On days like this one, the banana leaves glow. That's right, the sun goes right through them and the cool dark green turns bright and glows! And inside the glowing leaves there are dancing shadows from the other leaves of that same banana tree, as it dances in the breeze. It is like a leaf dance party. But when the rainy season stops, the glow goes away, and brown dust covers each leaf. Even in the rainy season, it is sunny every morning. The rain comes in the afternoon. So rainy season mornings are my favorite, because the leaves are so green in the morning sun.

Mama put more money in the secret drawer. She said that money will be for a stronger house someday and that maybe it would even have two rooms. I want to help save money for our new house, too, but I cannot work very much when I am in school. Once when I was out with Papa in the city, I saw boys and girls my age selling jasmine worship trinkets to people on the street. They were making money for their families.

"I can do that too, Papa!"

But Papa said they were so poor they had to quit school and do that. He said that I am smart and I should go to school. Then I can get a good job someday. He also said it is just not safe for those kids. I did notice that they had no Papas and Mamas with them. One boy even had a little skinny baby wrapped in a dirty old krama and tied across his body.

March 30, 1992
Ten years old

I am ten now and Sopheak is eight, so we help Mama a lot with the little ones. Sela helps too, but she is only seven. Sopheak has a really good heart. He is a good planner too. He thinks a lot. Sometimes I think he thinks too much though, and that makes him worry. He should have more fun.

Sela is the funny one. She makes the little ones and all the neighborhood kids laugh. One time, she learned about washing hands and other stuff about being clean at school, so she came right home and gathered the neighborhood kids together. Then she acted out about using the toilet and then eating with dirty hands because she was too lazy to wash her hands. That part was so funny! I laughed so hard I cried. Then she acted that she was sick from not washing, and I almost believed it. She held her stomach and rolled around on the ground moaning. She is a good actress, and she is only seven! Once I saw the actors on a TV at Uncle Reak's noodle shop, and I think Sela is funnier than they are. It's a crazy thing to say about your little sister who is only seven, but that's the truth!

Sokaa is five. He is starting to get into trouble. He thinks he can just go anywhere he wants anytime. Last week he went missing, and when we found him along the dirt-market road, he was hiding something in his pants. Mama was not home yet and Yay was sleeping. So, me and Sopheak, we picked him up; Sopheak held his feet and I held his arms. Then we shook him and some palm sugar candy fell out of his pant leg. We knew he stole it because of the way he was hiding it, but he just screamed like we were the ones being bad. He even kicked Sopheak in the mouth and made him bleed. We decided not to tell Mama. It was better for us just to deal with Sokaa by ourselves so Mama would not worry. Luckily, Mama was so busy with the cooking and minding the twins, she did not notice Sopheak's fat lip. The twins are only three. Malia and Mony are so cute and sweet I just want to eat them up!

They both have curly wispy black hair that tosses this way and that. They hate it when I comb their hair because it is always full of knots. But they never scream like Sokaa. They just make sad faces and let their tears drop from their big round black eyes, sitting straight and still like the stone Buddhas at the temple.

CHAPTER ELEVEN

Sophy

Almost everything that Sophy and Sret passed on the moto called out to her, as if she had a magic pair of glasses that caused her to see things through the eyes of a child. She wished she could leap off the bike and explore. Glistening golden temple roofs. Giant glowing banana leaves dancing in the wind. School children pumping the pedals of their too-big bicycles. Wooden houses on legs with tall ladder stairways. It seemed there were just two types of homes: wood and concrete. In general the further out they got from the city, the more were the number of wooden houses. Once she spotted workers bricking in the space under a wooden house on stilts, and she realized that this was how things progressed. If a family could get the money, they increased space by enclosing the space under the house.

Still trying to adjust to the heat, she'd asked, "Sret, which one is cooler to live in? Wooden or concrete houses?"

"Wood. The breeze flows through it at night and it gets cool without air conditioning."

"Hmm, amazing . . ." She nodded agreeably, but doubted this is her own mind.

Safe Space had rented Sophy's furnished apartment for interns. There was a hair salon on the ground level of the concrete building, and a *wat* (temple) two gates down the road. A guard had camped out in the shade of a faded Angkor Beer umbrella, his portable radio blaring traditional Khmai music. A narrow path of moldy terra-cotta tiles led to the stairway behind the salon. Yellow terrazzo stairs zig-zagged up the back of the building. Her place was on the fourth floor, which meant eight flights of stairs. Each flight had its own particular rises and treads that were utterly inconsistent. Combined with the rains that blew in, this made for dangerous entrances and exits. The lack of rhythm was unsettling since Sophy, a runner, was accustomed to trotting up and down stairs. A system of clear-story open-air grids and indoor windows connected each room with the next, and it had taken Sophy a while to see why that made sense. Airflow in that stifling heat meant survival. They had been given strict orders by Bethany to use the air-conditioning units in the bedrooms only at night. "It is super expensive. So get used to the heat."

The door opened into the kitchen. One long corridor led past the two carved wooden bedroom doors and opened out to a tiny living room, with a small balcony in the front. Grimy fans hung from the high ceilings in each room. When Sophy had asked about getting them cleaned, she was told, "It will look like that again in two weeks."

Sophy likened the *wats* to churches in the United States in that it seemed there was one on every corner. The grounds were usually full of trees, and the architecture was almost identical from one to another: gold trimmed buildings and high pointed roof lines, and adorned with Garuda birds and Naga snakes positioned as if holding the roofs up. Huge arched gateways opened to the grounds, where monks and school children poured in and out all day. Many of the *wats* were attached to the local school grounds. Every morning, she awoke to the sound of monks chanting over loudspeakers.

Based on her reading about Buddhism before she came, she'd imagined a peaceful melodic modulation. Instead, she was greeted each morning with a monotone cacophony. There were many beautiful aspects of the culture, but the chanting was not one of them in her opinion. She kept that thought to herself.

CHAPTER TWELVE

"What is a *bien*, Sret?" she casually asked from the back of the moto as they cruised down a country road on route to the safehouse. Every time they went from the office to the safehouse, they had to take a different route, in case any pimps tried to follow them. "I will show you," he called back to her. About ten minutes later, he pulled off the road at a little wooden shack. These longer rides on the moto made Sophy realize why cowboys walk bowlegged. She was still uneasy riding side saddle, so she straddled the bike. Pulling her helmet off her head for some reprieve from the heat, she re-did her low "helmet ponytail" to the top of her head and wiped the sweat from her neck with her *krama*. Then pulling the sweat soaked back of her jeans off her thighs, she shook out her legs and walked them out.

A small rack of two-liter glass soda bottles full of yellow liquid was stationed in front of the shack. "*Muey Lit.*" Sret ordered one liter of gas for his moto. The teenage boy flipped up the moto seat, screwed off the tank lid and turned the Fanta bottle upside down while it gurgled out. Sophy's mind drifted to the diary. She imagined little Kunthea, disguised in her demon-resistant braided hairdo, sniffing the gas fumes in the air, with delight.

A thick brown hand waved in front of her eyes. Sophy turned to see Sret, his familiar grinning face tilted to one side with one eye closed, clearly curious about the way she was zoning out. She laughed it off, and he motioned to Sophy to follow him. They walked around behind the shack, where there were two huge grey pots. Molded from fine concrete and polished smooth, they were full of water.

"These are *biens*." Instinctively knowing that she'd want to know more, he reached for a beat-up blue plastic bowl that was floating on the top of the water and poured the water over his hands. Next, he walked over to an old-fashioned rusty iron pump and began to crank the handle up and down. After about four screechy pumps, water began to flow through a blue PVC pipe into the first *bien*. "Every country house and even city houses that do not have running water, have *biens*. Sometimes they get filled like this, from a well pump, but sometimes they get filled from the rainwater. People catch it from their tin roofs." Then he scooped one more bowl full of water from the *bien* and began to hold it over her head. Sophy screamed and ran away while he beamed his giant smile. "But this is a Cambodian bath!"

CHAPTER THIRTEEN

On the way home from the safehouse, Sophy complained from the backseat of the moto, "This *krama* feels hot, Sret."

"That is because it is a fake one from China. Did you get it at Toul Tompoung, the tourists' market?"

"Yes."

"I will get you a real Cambodian cotton *krama* at Orussey Market. They make them on looms under their houses in the provinces. You'll have to wash it about five times to make it soft, and then it will feel perfect."

Her phone rang then. Pulling it from her bag, she wedged it inside her helmet. "Hello."

"Sophy, this . . . Phearun. You . . . come in again. We . . . fifteen more . . . today."

Between the broken signal and the moto engines and beeps that encompassed her, Sophy caught enough to know she should go to Lighthouse for more entries.

"Hi Ali! Phearun said to come in for more entries."

"Right. He will be back soon from the printer. Ours is down so he ran up the road to a shop. Have a seat!" Ali had that big brother thing going on again. And strangely, Sophy felt as if he really could be her big brother. She had never viewed herself as being Asian and always felt most comfortable with western people.

"Ali, can I ask you something?"

"Of course! How can I help?"

"I am just hoping you may be able to explain to me why everyone keeps saying I look Khmai but do not act Khmai. They make a big deal about it, like it is so obvious, but I cannot see why."

"Ah, I see. Well, you see native Khmai people have an attitude of deference and they carry themselves as such. But us westerners are more . . . How shall I say . . . assertive maybe?" Ali hesitated.

"What do you mean, assertive?" Sophy pressed.

"Well, think about the heroes in American films. What are they usually like?"

"Good question . . . I think they are . . . confident, strong, bold."

"Yes, you might put it that way, I suppose."

Sophy could see that Ali was skirting around something. "Is that not how other people see American heroes?"

Ali laughed, and Sophy began to see it. "So I guess confident and bold are just nice words for arrogant and in-your-face?"

"You are catching on, Sophy!"

"Wow . . . so does that mean people think I act *arrogant*?"

"Not necessarily, but Americans just carry themselves with a certain confidence."

Just then Phearun returned. He smiled gently as he handed her the next folder, as if a bit worried about her. As she was leaving, he asked, "Sophy, your parents are survivors of Pol Pot, is that right?"

"I think so, but they never talk about it. So maybe it was not so bad for them."

By the next morning, she knew why he'd asked.

KUNTHEA'S DIARY PART THREE

July 1, 1992
Ten years old

Da just mostly sits and stares out his window at the Mekong these days. He is not that old really, but sometimes he sits there like he could not move, the way a really old person does. I heard Mama talking with Aunt Mony while they were slicing cucumbers, "The memories have a grip on him." And I know now what they mean, because I am not a baby any more. It is the Pol Pot memories.

Now I know more about it. My friend Sokleak told me there is a museum in Phnom Penh about it. She said lots of people were killed by Pol Pot and his friends, when our parents were youth like us. Our parents and grandparents, they saw horrible things. Sometimes they lined them up by a big ditch and shot them all dead with guns, and their dead bodies just fell straight into the ditches. And sometimes they waited until they were almost starved first and then killed them. Now I understand why Mama tears up when she tries to talk about it. I think she actually wants to talk, but then it is really hard because of the memories. Sokleak said that, if someone surprises her Da, he tries to grab them, and one time he hurt a guy pretty badly before another man stopped him. When he realized what he did, he started to shake and cry and looked so ashamed. She told me she wanted to hold him and say it was not his fault, but instead she just left so he would not feel ashamed in front of her. Sokleak and I want to go see this museum. But we have to get the money for a romok cart, and Papa does not want me to go to the city without him. Someday we will go. I wonder if the

Pol Pot soldiers were all dead people who came back as animals, like tigers who just want to kill.

October 30, 1992
Ten years old

Last week I asked my teacher about the Pol Pot time. My teacher likes me because I work so hard and I am the top student in her class.

"Please wait Kunthea, and I will tell you." And then later, while the other children played outside, she sat on the front step with me.

She explained that the Pol Pot time was also called the Red Khmai. It was a communist revolution in Cambodia. They were tired of rich people controlling everything, so they tried to make everyone the same — farmers. It seemed like a good idea at first, that all people should be equal. But they believed that the rich and educated people would never learn to be equal, so they started killing them. At first, they killed people with guns, but they started to run out of bullets, so they started using farm tools like hoes and smashing people's heads with them. I felt sick when she said that, and she asked me if I'd heard enough. I asked her to please keep talking. If my yay and da and mama and papa lived through this, then I couldn't pretend it never happened. She said that the Red Khmai had trained youth, people my own age, to be soldiers and to kill people. She also said that they tried to take away all family connections and art and music. They even killed all the monks and shut down all of our beautiful golden temples. I felt angry and sad to think that this happened. I was not really hungry after that. I just sat thinking about how anyone could have that much power. And my teacher let me just sit there for a while, even when the playtime was over.

December 12, 1992
Ten years old

Today I saw Vannak's papa going out of Mrs. Seng's house again. He goes there a lot when she is home alone. But I won't say so. Last time I said so to Yay and she whacked me hard! She would have whacked me twice, but Papa walked in. He took me walking along the river. I was only nine then, but I knew enough to know that Vannak's papa had two wives: Vannak's mama and Mrs. Seng. Once I saw him run out the back door just before Mr. Seng got home.

"Why did Yay hit me, Papa?"

Papa knelt down in front of me on the muddy shore line, and explained, "Because she wants you to learn not to bring shame on others." He smiled and held my face in his big gentle hands, "I tell you what. When you see things that make you sad or angry, you can just tell me, and those things will be our secrets, ok?" I am so glad that my papa has just one wife: my mama.

May 15, 1993
Eleven years old

Today Sotheary and I were eating mien fruit at her house after school. Her Ming Tata was there and Sotheary boldly asked her to tell us what she remembered. I was surprised because Sotheary is usually kind of shy, but I think she is just tired of not knowing. Ming looked out her window to see who was around, and then she turned to us and took a deep breath and started talking.

"I was seven years old. Mama (Sotheary's yay) was pregnant. It was just me and Mama. They had taken Papa and my little brother,

Virak, away from us, on an oxcart. He was only three and he cried so hard to leave Mama. She tried to control herself for his sake, smiling like everything would be ok, but after the cart drove away, she turned and vomited in the brush. And then she sobbed but no sound came out for what seemed like forever. I will never forget the look on her face. That's what a broken heart looks like I think. Mama's face on that day."

Tata paused for a long moment. "Later on, we thought they were dead, but we did not know. It had been three months since we saw them. We were staying under the house of a farmer in a village. Mama and I had to work in the rice fields all day long, every day. The soldiers told Mama they would take me away too if she did not work harder. She just moved her arms harder but there was no emotion in her face. It had left with Papa and the baby. We did not have enough to eat. Just a small cup of rice each day. Mama was too thin. She looked like a sugar palm tree trunk with one round coconut sticking out of it.

"One night, Mama woke me up and whispered, her face right up to mine, 'Listen, Tata, be quiet as a rat and follow me.' We carefully snuck away from the village, through the rice paddy and into the forest. Mama had one large *krama* bundled onto her back, with some cassava root and sugar palm juice for us. Normally we would walk along the dirt dikes between the rice fields, but this time we had to run with our heads low, right through the fields. One soldier, who was supposed to keep watch, had fallen asleep next to the oxcarts. Mama told me later that she had seen him drinking rice wine, and she soon figured out he did that every night. That made him even more scary to me. The only thing worse than a Pol Pot soldier was a drunk one. We knew that. But to Mama it meant that he would sleep harder. We snuck past him, hiding behind a sleeping water buffalo. Right when I went by, it moved its giant head and snorted! The night sky was glowing blue behind his huge black horns, as they slowly raised up from the mucky earth. I stopped and stared as they hung silhouetted over me. I held my breath and almost screeched out a cry, but Mama suddenly dropped to her knees in front of me, took my hand and squeezed it hard, saying with her hand and her eyes what she could not voice. 'Our lives depend on you not making a sound.'"

Ming Tata just stopped talking then. I looked at Sotheary and she just made big eyes at me and grimaced. It seemed like forever we all three just sat there, and I could not even look at Tata. Then she got up and checked out the window again. She settled back down on the mat slowly, painfully, like each thought in her head hurt right now and it slowed her whole body. As I watched her, I thought how beautiful she is, with big almond brown eyes, the kind that hold a big pool of tears in the rims, before they spill down the face. Her hair is soft and wavy, and she lets it hang that way. Some Khmai ladies try to straighten their hair, but Tata does not care if it is curly, and I like it that way.

She began again, "We walked for days, and soon we were in the mountains. At night Mama would gather some leaves and try to make us a bed of them. We laid there holding on to each other, trying to sleep. But I do not remember ever sleeping, because one time, I was watching the tree branches above us, and one of them moved, growing fatter and longer until I saw the shape. A tiger. He posed there on that branch like a statue, then suddenly leapt to the next branch and I gasped and closed my eyes and clenched my teeth, sure he would come to eat us. After that, I laid awake every night with my eyes wide open, fixed on the trees above us.

"Mama found leaves for us to eat, but some of them were so bitter. After three days of running, Mama started to have pain in her belly. It was not time for the baby to come yet, but by night fall, it did.

Mama gritted her teeth but would not scream, no matter how she hurt. I had never helped birth a baby, because I was just a little girl. There was so much blood, I thought Mama would die and I'd be left there all alone. The baby was a boy. He was too small. His skin was very thin and falling from his body. He did not cry or move, and I knew — he was dead. I sat there holding his tiny little body and stared at his face, his perfect little face, the tiny flat nose that would never breathe, his little full lips that would never suckle. Mama rolled over on the bed of leaves I had made her, and she muffled her sobs in the leafy dirt. I sat on the ground holding my dead baby brother, thinking of what to do. Then I heard it, something moving through the leaves. Tigers. I didn't even try to see them, but I heard, a deep growling purr, like a street cat but one with the power to eat people, not just mice. The sound was so close. I thought my heart would stop beating right then, but I had to be strong for Mama. This time I was the one who had to be brave: I laid the baby down in the leaves and rolled Mama towards me. Grabbing her shoulders tight I put my face right up to hers and whispered hard, 'Tigers. We have to run!' She nodded through her tears while I helped her up and we fled that place, leaving my dead baby brother behind, for the tigers to eat."

Then Ming Tata covered her mouth with her hand, sucked in her breath and choked out some sobs. Her huge eyes pinched shut and the tears poured down her face. I thought Sotheary should tell her to stop talking, but she did not. I looked at the floor, not knowing how to feel. Tata turned her teary face towards the window and paused for a long time. "So now you know why Mama is not right. No woman should ever have to abandon her child to tigers, even if he is dead."

Now Sotheary's yay is known in our village for suddenly standing in people's doorways and staring at them. You do not know anyone is there, and then you see the shadow she creates on the floor of your hut. Some people even call her "the ghost" when she is not around. I wonder what happens in the heart and soul of someone like her. Does she somehow think that her baby is in another house somewhere? Will she wander around looking for him in the afterlife too? Where is his spirit? He did not have any time to do anything bad or good. He was born dead.

Ming Tata went on, "After two more days of walking, we reached our village in Takao Province. Papa and baby Virak were not there. Papa came home one month later, without Virak. Mama screamed and sobbed and hit Papa. She could not even look at him. 'Why didn't you watch him? How could you lose him? Didn't you try to find us?'

"Mama would not be near him, and when she walked away, I saw his big shoulders shaking and his head hanging down. None of us talked about it for a long time, but Mama forgave Papa after a while, and one night while the crickets sang, I heard them talking and crying softly together under their net. Papa said Virak strayed from him in the forest just before dark, and he looked for him for two days and nights.

"He whispered through his tears, '*Oun*, I'm afraid the tigers ate him.'

"So, Mama lost two boys to tigers. Tigers and Pol Pot."

My Mama is pregnant now. I almost wish I did not know Tata's story. Whenever I look at Mama and her baby belly, I think of Sotheary's yay birthing her dead baby in the forest and leaving it to the tigers. And last night I did not sleep much because I was afraid of dreaming about that. It felt better just to lay awake. I made up my mind to scold the village kids when they make fun of Sotheary's yay.

January 17, 1994
Twelve years old

Click click click. I rolled over and listened to the rhythm of Mama's spoon in her batter bowl. The crickets were still singing in the old mango tree, and the boats softly bumped against the docks down on the river. I scooted to the top edge of my mat and peered through the floor slats. By the light of the lantern, she whisked in the rice four and it puffed out onto her gold sarong.

She said Papa is not bringing home as much money as before. So, Mama wakes up at 4:00 a.m. now and is making noom goam (snack made with coconut and rice flour) before she goes to school. I am in the morning session now and home by noon, so I walk the streets and the village market to sell the *noom*. My neighbor Mrs. Seng taught me how to roll my *krama* into a neat little circle, twisting it as I go, and tucking the end into the wreath nice and tight. With the *krama* wreath right on top my head, the big flat basket balances there easily. I just have to rearrange the *noom* each time I sell some, or the balance will be off.

February 10, 1994
Twelve years old

As I moved through the market with my head basket, triangles of dust-filled orange sunlight poured in and weaved around the stalls. There was a gust of powerful wind, and suddenly the market was filled with dust. Gritty dust. And smoke. In that moment, I thought, grilled fish does not usually smell like that. Then I heard someone screaming from the river bank. Then more screams. I squinted and fought my way towards the sounds. There from the last stalls on the westernmost edge of our market, I saw it through the haze — fire.

Scooped up by the hands of the wind and tossed along, the grass huts blossomed into flame one by one. *Poof poof poof.* My head basket fell to the ground. Someone had bumped into me, but I sat there frozen. The children! It seemed as though I was in a tunnel after that. I could not see on either side of me, only straight ahead. Grabbing my *krama*, I ran screaming, "Malia! Mony! Sela!" Gasping for air and choking down sobs, I imagined them helplessly trapped in the house, crying out for me. "Mony! Malia!"

Dark smoke gusted around corners. Everything was toppling; fish flopped about in the dirt, dry rice scattered on the market floor and rats scurried for cover. The powerful wind stirred it all in one swoop, Mamas and Papas, dust, children, smoke, chickens. Through the hazy smoke I saw a teen grabbing fruit from an abandoned stall. Another gust of blackened wind woke me from the scene to refocus. *Stop blowing! I need to find my little ones.*

On the dirt road and running on little barefoot legs, a small figure emerged through the dusty smoke; I knew that silhouette, curly strands of angel hair whipping about above her stalky little figure. The familiar little limp since she had cut her right foot two weeks before. Malia! My sweet Malia! Running at full speed I caught her in my arms. As she threw her little arms around my neck and squeezed her legs around my waist, I kept moving north. Slipping on the dirt, I rounded the corner left at Sotheary's house. Nothing. I looked toward my house but it was just a wall of smoke, dust and flame, rising up. Setting Malia's little feet down, I dropped to my knees, peering beneath the heavy veil, and catching a sob in my throat again.

"It hurts my eyes, *bong!*" Malia cried.

I tried to reply but the smoke caught in my throat. "Keep your eyes shut, *b'oan.* I've got you."

Closing and opening my eyes again, the sting was unbearable. But beneath the heavy veil, and through the fiery haze another figure emerged. No, two . . . now three. Sopheak! Mony and Sela! Breathless and smudged black, Sopheak coughed out, "Run . . . no one there!" Grabbing the little ones, we leapt towards the high road. Glancing right, we caught sight of the market, already engulfed and swallowed by flames that reached for the sky. Without a word, we headed for the main road two more blocks east. People swarmed the street. Some were passers-by pushing in to see what was happening. Mostly people were screaming out names. We headed south towards *Oam* Reak's noodle shop. The sun was setting over the Mekong now. In a fog of faces and dust, I glanced back. A huge black tower of smoke rose up over my little fishing village, laced by sparkling orange threads of firelight set against the deepening blue of evening sky. Just then, the factory romoks came tumbling towards us. Realizing that the smoke came from their village, the women returning from the factory, who usually sat properly around the edges of the carts, their hair neatly tucked up under their sunhat *kramas*, were bursting forth, leaping from the romoks before they even stopped, screaming out for their children. In a sea of desperate rushing eyes, we searched for the face of our own mama. She should have been walking home from the school then, too, but no one was just walking. Too many mamas ran past us.

I hung my head, sucked in the gritty air and stood there shaking with fear. It was then that I realized — we did not have Sokaa. How could I face Mama without all her babies saved? Anger burned inside me as I thought of Sokaa, and the way he disobeys. He should have been at the house with Sopheak. Was he out stealing candy again?

"Kunthea!"

Swinging around, I fell into Mama's arms. We all sputtered and stammered but couldn't say a thing. Her eyes darted to each child, and she knew Sokaa was missing. But Mama was so brave. The tears began to flow but she never stopped. She picked up Malia and led us on. It was two more streets to Oam's house. I prayed the others would be there.

Yay and Da were already there with Sokaa, and when I saw his big eyes glistening at me over Da's shoulder, I cried and wiped his blackened face with my *krama*. The little guy was coughing and listless, not at all his usual self. I remembered writing about his endless naughty energy in my diary — my diary! For a moment I thought it had burned up along with my village, all the memories erased from the pages forever! That thought stole any strength I had left, and I collapsed against the wall. But something cushioned my fall, and I realized it was my backpack! It had been on me all along and I did not even know it. Scrambling to get it off, I opened the rusty zipper and there it was. My diary was safe. Like everything and all of us, it smelled like smoke, but it was safe. I rolled onto my side and cried knowing I'd not even care about my diary if Papa was gone.

Five hours later, we were all together. Papa was the last one to come. He had stopped to help many others find their loved ones. Smudged black with soot and sweat, he stumbled through the gate at Oam's at 11:00 p.m., dropped to his knees and sobbed as we all piled onto him.

February 11, 1994
Twelve years old

The smell of everything smoldering caught in my throat and stung my eyes, so I had to keep stuffing my *krama* in my face. Nothing is left. Ninety-five homes were lost. Papa took me and Sopheak with him, and we walked slowly through the charred rubble of our village. Papa called to us to be careful and to stay away from the little threads of black smoke that curled up in the smoggy air. He said it was still hot there and we could get burned.

Aunt Mony sat on a half-burned wood stump, crying and holding a picture frame. Sotheary's aunt Tata stood in her sarong, staring out towards the Mekong, with the blackened remains of their spirit house at her feet. I wondered if she was thinking about her niece who drowned in the Mekong or her baby brothers who were eaten by tigers. Where were their spirits now with no spirit house to stay in?

And I was glad that Yay and Da were not with us to see this. We would figure this out for us and for them. Da was already haunted by his memories from the Pol Pot time. He did not need more.

March 9, 1994
Twelve years old

We stayed at Oam's in the back for two weeks. The space was tiny for all nine of us. Yay and Da slept in the house, but we were out with the mosquitos. At least it is dry season so we are not wet.

April 8, 1994
Twelve years old

Papa got wood from some of the people he has helped in the past, a little from one and more from another until we had enough to build a new house. The roof tilts one direction for the rain to run off. There is only one wall. We used to have eight meters by twenty meters for our house and Da and Yay's. We had to sell the front ten meters, and we lost the road access. The people are building a concrete house there. One side of our house is open to their wall that protects us a little from wind and rain. There were no long pieces for stilts, so the house is short with a small ladder to climb up on the platform. Papa feels ashamed of the new house. Sometimes he is angry when he thinks about how all our money burned up with the house. The key in Mama's secret bra pocket was no good after the table burned up. Sometimes he is angry and sometimes just sad. Really sad. So, he drinks. He drinks and loses the money from his police work. Some he spends on the beer, but more on gambling. He keeps telling Mama, "Next time, oan, and I will win. Then we will have enough money."

It is early April, but no one is celebrating yet. Khmai New year will come and go this year. Our whole village is rebuilding their lives. The teachers said we can have Khmai New Year games at school this year. I do not even know which angel comes this year, and I do not care.

May 18, 1994
Twelve years old

I knew it was wrong, but I sobbed and screamed at Papa right there in the Chinese hospital. I even hit him. They were shaving Mama to take the baby.

"She is too weak. You must choose who to keep alive. The mother or the baby." It rung in my ears. *The mother or the baby . . . the mother or the baby . . .*

Then he said it. Blankly, Papa said it like it meant nothing, without even stopping to think. Quiet but clear. "The baby."

"You have six babies and only one wife!" I sobbed and choked. He just sat and stared out the window at the smoky black night, while Mama moaned through her last breaths. Casting its shadow across the floor, a huge cockroach scurried by me. A single dim light bulb hung from a cord, so I could barely see the scummy walls. But I knew how dirty that place was from the smell. And the roaches. I fell to my knees and dropped my head against a broken plastic chair, not caring if a million roaches climbed on me, because Mama was about to die.

I could not look at Papa. The electricity went off while they were taking the baby, and I heard the doctors yelling. I thought surely they both would die. Mosquitos buzzed in and out of the window. A sliver of weak blue light shone through the open bars from one florescent bulb on battery from the house across the alley. Some drunken men stopped to pee on the wall below, joking around as if nothing important was happening inside. The stench of the urine grew stronger in the absence of fans and sweat dripped down my back.

Finally, a nurse came out, "It is a girl and the mother is still alive."

I ran in to Mama and she was breathing, but so weak and so pale. And my baby sister was so tiny, quiet, sleeping in a dirty worn blanket. The sight of her somehow caught my breath. Now seeing her, I felt sorry for Papa. How could they ask him to decide? It is too hard a question for anyone to answer. Her tiny hands gripped the blanket, grasping, but holding on to what? A hope of nothing? How would I take care of her after Mama died? I barely even have breasts and they have no milk for a baby. I wanted to die myself. I turned away and vomited in the trash can.

January 15, 1995
Thirteen years old

I told her today, Miss Sophia, that I would look for a factory job and lie about my age. And quit school. She said she knew this day would come, but when I said it she swallowed hard and tears pooled up in her light brown eyes.

"You are so smart, Kunthea. You must stay in school." She had reminded me over and over. How did she know this day would come?

I had rehearsed the speech in my head the entire way to school. "Only for a while . . . We hope . . . Mama says . . . We just can't make it with Mama so sick and not working, and now Papa drinking." No, I cannot tell her that part. It is too shameful. The dread hung over me like huge shadows of ghosts I could not see.

Entering the school yard, I suddenly awoke from my thoughts in a moment of panic, and then relief, to see that Sopheak, Sela and Sokaa were still there, kicking up the dust ahead of me. But it was the walk home that I could not bear. When would I hear these sounds again, ever — the clicking of the bicycle wheels, the boys calling out in teasing rhymes? Would Sela still tell me all about her day when I get home late from a factory job? Or would she tire by then and forget the colorful stories we used to share on the dusty road home?

"Kunthea! Come on!" Sela and Sokaa skipped through the schoolyard gate, but I had stopped and turned back to see it. Shielding my eyes from the sun, I glanced back at Sopheak. He nodded at me knowingly while he tousled Sokaa's hair.

Turning towards home, he took their hands on either side, "Did I ever tell you the story about my friend . . .?"

I stood there facing the three single-story faded yellow concrete buildings that made up our school. They surround the dirt play yard, like a little fortress meant to protect us and help us grow safely, and the statue of the boy and girl in the blue and white school clothes, holding hands, stepping forward towards life and learning. On my first day of school, I thought they were me and Sopheak. I still do. And I imagined the boy, all alone. And I gulped and blinked back my tears. I walked through the gate one last time, into my new life without school.

Mr. Vuen told Mama about a shoe factory where his niece works.

January 18, 1995
Thirteen years old

Seven *mearn riel*: seventeen dollars and fifty cents each month. Two dollars and fifty cents go to the *romok* driver, so that leaves fifteen. We start at 7:00 a.m. and work until 5:00 p.m., six days a week. This week, I have one main goal: remember my name is Radee and I am eighteen years old, not thirteen-year-old Kunthea. We had to lie so I could get the job. Most of the workers are under eighteen.

Mr. Chong screamed, "Radee!" his stinky fish breath filing my nose. I had not responded the first time, because my name is Kunthea. But my cousin is Radee; she is eighteen and I am her now. He screams at us in Chinese as if we will understand. And today he hit my friend Vuthy, because she was too slow. Vuthy and I use our stencils to cut the leather pieces for the shoes. But the machine blade is so sharp and she is afraid. I am afraid too, but I have learned the rhythm of the cutter. Like music, it has a timing.

Two hundred shoes a day — that is the new quota. If we do not meet it, we work overtime with no pay. I am so afraid Vuthy will not be able to keep up.

May 5, 1995
Thirteen years old

Da talked about Pol Pot. He just sat there and stared out his window. And he told me terrible things. I wanted him to stop, but he just kept talking, low and soft, and I knew it would be so disrespectful to leave and not listen. So I listened because I respect my Da, but more because I love him. He said that he escaped over to Thailand. Mama was sixteen and her sister, Aunt Liang, was eighteen. They were with him and Yay. He said the Thais took Uncle Hak and the other one from him, and they made them cross the border, back into Cambodia. Da never says the name of the other one, but I know Da lost a son to Pol Pot. He said that Hak and the other one hid in the jungle for two days . . . And Da and Yay were sure they were dead. Then the Pol Pot soldiers found them and made them run through a field of land mines while they shot at them with guns. The other one was killed by their bullets or a landmine or both. Hak said he could not look back, so he never really knew, and sometimes he wondered if he was killed at all, that maybe he was alive somewhere. After two years in the refugee camp in Thailand, Uncle Hak went to live in Minnesota and he never came home. Da said they chose Uncle Hak to go, because he was strong and he could get good work in America and send money back to them.

Da got some tears in his eyes when he said that and he stopped talking for a long time but I could not leave him, because he was not finished. I felt a big lump in my throat and I wanted to cry. We just sat there, and I tried to chase the pictures from my head of Uncle Hak and his brother running through the fields with the Red Khmai running after them, shooting. And I remember that Mama said there was no school for them either, just work and more work and not enough food to eat. And I thought, things have not changed, except now no one is shooting us. And then, there in the painful silence with Da, I imagined my lost uncle was standing in the doorway and Da was weeping with joy because his son was alive.

Then Da talked some more until he was not angry, or sad, or anything. His old eyes just stayed fixed there on the Mekong as the sun set over it. I listened while the sun set, turning his leathery skin from whitish grey to deep orange pink, and the shadows filled the deep lines on his forehead and around his old eyes. Then it was dark, but there was no power in the darkness, just sadness and quiet. I did drop some tears then, but Da did not see them.

Da's stories about Pol Pot are just too much for me right now. I have so many problems now. Mama is so weak; the baby is hungry because she can hardly nurse her. I have sworn with myself to never tell Mama that Papa told the doctors to save the baby and not her. It is a secret she just does not need to know. I do not want to know it, but I do. Papa has kept my secrets, so I can keep his.

September 18, 1995
Thirteen years old

"Do not let Sokaa and the twins bathe in the Mekong. It is too high and dangerous." Sopheak and I reviewed the daily responsibilities in the dawn's dim light before I left for work. He nodded plainly. As the romok pulled away, I looked back at him standing limply by the edge of the road. He looked so thin, like a tiny soft leaf, he could be carried away himself at any moment. He used to grow so fast. He ran and played, and he ate so much. My dear Sopheak, he worried when there was nothing to worry about. How will he survive when there is? And he is only eleven.

September 25, 1996
Fourteen years old

They moved me to the dye-color spraying section on the third floor today. The smell of the dye makes me dizzy. Vuthy is cleaning the floors now, because she was still too slow on the machines. I miss her. Even though we could rarely talk, her soft eyes would speak to me above her soiled mask. They said we would be ok.

The bell rang. I let the crowd carry me as we poured out onto the road. Five kilos thinner than when I began at the factory, I sometimes have the feeling of floating with the crowds. And yet, somehow I feel heavy. I used to rush out through the gate, eager to fill my empty belly with rice at the lunch bell. I did not even care about the layer of road dust that settled over my small plastic bowl full, or even the occasional long black hairs. It was the cramping and diarrhea that made me lose my appetite. Now the grit as I chew makes me nauseated. A sea of light blue head scarves and long black ponytails spread out before me like ants after food crumbs, and I searched for Vuthy. She keeps her hair in a bun under her scarf, so it does not fall into the mop water. She cleans on floor two now, far from Mr. Chong, and I am glad she feels safer.

Each bin is seventy-five kilos. Mr. Chong makes us drag them to the holding room. But now I am too weak.

CHAPTER FOURTEEN

Sophy

The three cups of coffee she drank that morning made her jittery. Sophy's hand shook while she tried to type. But it was no use. She could not get the stories out of her head. She'd read until 3:00 a.m.

"I am not feeling well, so I am going to go home." She told the staff she'd catch up tomorrow. Kunthea was shaking her world, and she was almost regretting having found the diary. The excitement of discovery had turned to a cautious yet curious dread. But it was too late to turn back.

On her way home, Sophy burst into tears under her helmet visor. Images of the life she'd had growing up, contrasted with the life of Kunthea, were dancing in her head, and she couldn't turn it off.

Sophy's parents' beliefs were a mystery to her. They had a small shrine, much like what Kunthea had described as a spirit house. She'd hated the smell of the incense and was embarrassed to have friends over. Her mother also wore a small gold cross necklace and would rub it between her fingers and pray. Sophy knew she was praying to Buddha, but her mother had said the cross was "just in case" because many people in America worshipped Jesus. This way she was honoring Buddha and Jesus.

The rain became heavier, so she pulled into the Bokor Caltex, under the overhang to wait it out. They had just reopened the gas station, but not the coffee shop. Sophy took off her helmet and sat straddling the Chaly as she watched the heavy veil of rain. As the torrent escalated, every available space filled in with others seeking shelter, and she had the strange feeling that others might hear her thoughts, because the stories were so big and loud. They were the kind you cannot ignore — the fire, Aunt Tata's story of birthing a dead baby in the jungle or being forced to quit school. The roar of the rain helped drown out the loudness, at least so others could not hear her heart beating like she could.

Sophy remembered walking to the public library after school in Ohio, a beautiful huge building full of colorful books you could borrow for free. The landscaping was pristine: emerald green grass and manicured spring flowers. She remembered Kunthea standing at the gate of her school for the last time, surrendering her education for her family's survival. And she wondered if she would have ever loved her parents like that. Back at her place, she climbed back into bed and cried herself to sleep.

Later that afternoon, she called Sret, "Can you take me to a school, Sret? Do all schools have statues of little boys and girls in the yard?"

CHAPTER FIFTEEN

Two weeks later, Sophy had pulled herself back into focus, in part by distracting herself with other things. She and some friends took a trip to see Angkor Wat, the famous ancient temple site in Siem Reap.

A young mom plopped down in the seat in front of them on the bus. Heavy plastic bags bulging with fresh fruit hung from her right hand, as she balanced a toddler on her other hip. The boy looked to be about two years old. Grabbing onto the seat back, he began to climb, scaling like a pro, and Sophy realized why this mom looked a bit worn out.

"*Choap, Choap! Som-doh,*" she winced at Sophy.

"*Aught Ai! Go'at jia broh toamada.*" Sophy smiled. She looked at Matthias and laughed. He smiled back and waited.

"Oh, right. Sorry! She told the baby to stop climbing and apologized to us. I said it's ok; he is just being a normal boy."

Matthias exchanged a glance and a smile with the mom, who responded by thrusting a small open plastic bag towards him. Sophy looked inside, and smiled, "It's fried crickets. She is offering you a snack."

Rescuing him from the awkward moment, Sophy reached into the bag and took out a few of the crispy seasoned crickets. "*Aw-kgun!* Thank you!"

As the little boy grabbed for the bag, Sophy popped a cricket into her mouth, and Matthias' mouth hung open.

"You *are* Khmai!" he teased. At first the words stung, but Sophy laughed. "They taste like crispy chicken."

Matthias gave her a one-sided, doubt-filled half grin, the kind when he tilted his head and closed one of his green sapphire eyes.

She defended her claim, "Honest! They do!" and she tried shoving one in his mouth.

When Matthias smiled like that, Sophy had to fight falling for him.

Don't be so immature, Sophy. Just because he is so hot. And he is too young anyway. She had dated several guys before, and they looked awesome, too. But she knew Matthias was different. He was so focused on doing stuff that matters, he did not even notice when women swooned at his looks. And that is what made not falling for him hard. That and his eyes, and his smile and . . . She shifted her focus on to settling in for the six-hour ride.

CHAPTER SIXTEEN

Phearun had suggested she take ear phones unless she loved blaring Khmai karaoke music. Sure enough, the bus had a heavy-looking old TV up front, hanging from a precariously rigged frame of metal. It was about five times louder than it needed to be. Everyone but the foreigners seemed to enjoy this. Matthias put on his Bose noise-blocking headphones and dozed off. Sophy's earbuds were not so effective, but she managed for a while to block out the chaos.

Her thoughts wandered back to the international supermarket in Cleveland, Ohio, about a forty-minute drive from where they lived. It was a weird hybrid of what she'd seen at the open-air Cambodian markets and a modern US supermarket. Of course, it was not open air because of the winters there. Instead, there were little stalls all around the edges where immigrants from various countries made fresh ethnic food. The pungent smell of exotic spices filled the air, and to young Sophy they all smelled good. She loved listening to the workers at each stall, calling out orders and instructions in several different languages, each with its own special cadence and sounds that were nothing like English. The languages were exotic, too, and she'd even thought once that English sounded boring. But these were the kind of thoughts she'd kept to herself. That is where Sophy learned to eat fried crickets. Matthias was right. She was Khmai despite all her efforts to not be.

It seemed to take forever to get out of Phnom Penh. The driver would stop at random spots along the road and pick up or drop off more people. Finally, even the aisleway was blocked. Red plastic chairs materialized and were filled with travellers and their stuff. The strong smell of durian fruit wafted through the now cool bus. The AC units were old but powerful, and Sophy wondered why make it so cold that everyone needs jackets. Huge monsoon-made potholes made the bus lean from side to side and then lurch as it climbed out of each hole. This made reading impossible, so she surrendered and listened to her music and played peek-a-boo with the toddler until he drifted off to sleep.

Once they got out to the countryside, Sophy turned to watch out the window. The rains had flooded the rice fields, which were the most intense green she'd ever seen. The ever-present morning sun danced on the drenched fields as little sprouts poked through the smooth glassy surface. Sugar palm trees sprouted out from the ridges and spaces between the fields, sometimes in rows and sometimes in clusters. Their perfect reflections rested on the mirror-like fields.

Coal-black water buffalos emerged from murky ponds. Sun-glistened water spilled off their massive bodies. Others stayed submerged in the coolness, only snouts and huge horns poking up. Dingy ropes hung from their necks, the other end held by a scrappy little boy who needed a haircut. The contrast between the boy and his beast was astounding, partly because such a diminutive family member had been charged with the care, and partly because of the buffalo's massive hulk and the boy's utter lack of concern over leading it by a rope. She'd heard that a collision with one of these animals did more harm to a car than to the buffalo.

Short wood slatted bridges with no railings reached over roadside gulley ways filled with the monsoon rains. Huge flat lotus leaves floated on the surface, with occasional stalks of pink flowers sticking straight up, some budded and some in full bloom. Sophy thought the budded ones looked a bit like the tulips in Ohio in the early Spring. Each bridge led to two, three or more houses on stilts. Skinny white cows with humps on their backs stood like statues under the shade of the houses — nothing like the fat brown furry cows of Ohio. She had to look twice to see that they were cows at all. The nicest houses were wood, painted blue with traditional clay tile roofs and a small porch. But some houses were walled and roofed with dried leaves, with only open rectangular holes for doors and windows. And she thought about the houses of Kunthea's village going up in flames.

Sophy realized that she'd never asked her parents where they were from. A village? Phnom Penh? Another town? With a pang of guilt, she reached for her bag, pulled out her phone and typed a text.

"Hi Mama and Papa. Did I tell you that I have this really great driver who watches out for my safety all the time? So please do not worry about me. I am fine."

CHAPTER SEVENTEEN

"Have you been to Toul Sleng or the Killing Fields?" Matthias was awake again.

"No, not sure I want to go." Sophy knew about the genocide museums, and now Kunthea was making her even more curious. Perhaps Kunthea was braver than she. Perhaps Kunthea really wanted to know why her parents wouldn't talk.

Perhaps it would be easier to stay irritated with her parents, than to understand them.

Matthias challenged, "Well, who can really say they *want* to go there? It is not exactly a happy thing."

The bus stopped for a break in Kampong Thom, so they all got a table and ordered some fried rice and iced coffees. This trip was a good chance to slow down and take in Cambodia. Sophy had been hit through all of her senses when she'd first arrived. But frankly, it was overwhelming, so she'd sort of blocked things out, focusing on understanding one or two things at a time. It was as if she could only take in what she was learning from Kunthea, like her eyes were opened one step at a time. Like Kunthea looking for her family during the fire, she could only see what mattered right at the moment.

As they entered the open-air restaurant, they passed a huge shrine with little clay pots of burning incense. She stopped and looked. Offerings included a bunch of bananas and some noodle soup. A cup of sweet milk coffee had formed a film on the surface as the flies buzzed around it. And there were little statues. One was the sitting Buddha with the hood of the seven-headed Naga snake hanging over him for shelter. Some statues had multiple arms, and there were two fat little painted figurines of old men with long white beards. These did not look Khmai. She made a mental note to add these statues to her list of questions for Sret and Phearun.

A pineapple seller was whittling the eyes out of whole pineapples, in perfect diagonal ridges, making a huge pile of the outer rinds at her feet. A diaper-less baby wearing only a t-shirt sat on a grass mat gnawing the last bit of fruit off one of the rinds. The aroma of the incense combined with the already fermenting rinds filled her senses. She realized this was the smell of Cambodia that she had been unable to describe before.

Back on the bus, Sophy got drawn into the karaoke videos. They were stories. The singer, a handsome young Khmai guy, strolled mournfully through a rice field, crooning a love song as oxcarts lumbered by. It seemed like the *krama* tied around his head was meant to give him a country-boy look, but was a bit too clean. He flashed back to happier days. A beautiful girl twirled in his arms. They laugh and share ice cream by the Independence Monument. Then suddenly an older man and woman approach the couple and angrily grab her by the wrist and drag her away, as both she and the young man reach out for one another, crying. Next thing you know, the girl, dressed up and trying to look happy, is reluctantly escorted to a shiny black Land Rover in front of a gold-trimmed mansion. A young man clad in designer clothes and gold jewellery is in the driver's seat, but his focus seems to be on his car and his phone more than her. She is a reluctant bride, her parents smiling and nodding their approval of the match. Her country boyfriend watches in the background, tears streaming down his face. She catches a glimpse of him, and he flees on his moto, to his untimely death on the road. Three videos later, Sophy gave up hoping for a happy ending, put her earbuds in and took in the scenery.

CHAPTER EIGHTEEN

The following weekend, she went to Toul Sleng. By herself, Sophy walked the grounds of what had once been a city high school. Several three-story buildings stood on the grounds, which were surrounded by a typical stucco wall topped with barbed wire. Had Sophy only visited briefly, like the tourists, she'd have assumed the barbed wire was owing to the fact that it had been a prison during the Khmai Rouge, what Kunthea called the Pol Pot time. But in fact, all city homes had such walls for security purposes. Like the bars on windows, it was about keeping people out, not in.

She made it past the bloodstained rooms of two foot by two foot brick cells with iron shackles chained to the walls. There were paintings of victims being tortured, the list of rules and sickening consequences. It was the faces she could not take, rows and rows of mugshots of the victims. Faces that looked way too much like herself . . . and her parents. She'd made up her mind to not cry, so she got sick instead. Running from the room into the sun-filled dirt yard, she vomited.

CHAPTER NINETEEN

"The grounds at the safehouse are flooded and it will not get better until November at the earliest. We need rubber boots for the guard and for the girls when they do chores. There is no getting around the fact that there is sewage in the flood water, so it is a health issue." Bethany sent Jessica and Sophy out with Sret in the tuk-tuk.

Orussey Market was three tall stories high and three city blocks square. It was an economic center for locals, not a tourist market. At 3:00 a.m., old motos pulling flatbed carts were pulling up around all four sides. By the light of the moon and single street lamps, drivers and sellers met to exchange goods and cash: fifty-kilo bags of fresh garlic and cucumbers, thirty kilos of raw cashewnuts from Kampong Thom Province, sacks of avocados from Mondohl Kiri and weavers from Takao Province delivering uncut red checked cotton *kramas*, neatly tied in bundles of thirty meters each, which was roughly twenty *kramas*.

"What do they sell at Orussey, Sret?" Sophy inquired.

"Everything."

Three beat-up greasy motos pulled up in front of them, blocking the already-crowded street outside the market. Like other drivers who delivered goods to this market, their heads were wrapped in dusty old kramas. They wore grease-stained jeans and thin worn rubber flip flops that looked as though they'd fall off any moment. Whatever colors and designs that may have originally adorned their long-sleeved cotton shirts were now dulled with the dust from the road. This layer of dust on everything, combined with her recent reading, had made Sophy wonder what lay behind the dust. The original colors and patterns were like clues to be unearthed, veiled entrances into whole new worlds of stories.

Each moto had a cylindrical bamboo basket strapped tightly to the rack, and each basket contained one live squealing pig. One by one they hoisted these pig-laden baskets atop metal pallets on the ground. Opaque grey water with floating organic matter and trash sloshed about the grates. A seller, who seemed to materialize out of nowhere, pulled out wads of Khmer riel cash and handed it over, while others loaded the goods and disappeared into the dark recesses of the market. Sophy and Jessica covered their ears and winced at the intensely loud squeal of the pigs, and Sret laughed at them.

"Call me when you leave the market and I will pull up."

He had been scanning for a semi-dry piece of road where he could drop them off. Giving up, he pulled up as close as he could get. Not sure how deep it was, Sophy and Jessica stepped slowly out of the tuk-tuk into the murky flooded street, and sloshed their way to an entrance.

Once inside, they began to weave through the crowded dark aisleways. Random oscillating fans hung from precarious mounts, giving soft buzzing relief from the odors and heat. Voices murmured, "*Barang* (foreigner)," and Sophy knew they were talking about Jessica. She was the only white-skinned, blonde-haired person in the whole chaotic scene. Jessica had not learned that word yet and she was busy tracking behind Sophy, so she was blissfully unaware of her notoriety. Sophy decided to leave it that way.

In the maze of noise and confusion, they found themselves face to face with pig parts hanging from hooks.

"Disembodied pig snouts. Not what we are looking for," Sophy joked when she noticed Jessica looking a bit green.

Turning the corner abruptly, she bumped right into an entire pig's head. And yes, it was smiling at her.

Another flashback to Kunthea's world.

Sixteen wrong turns and five stops to ask for help later, they found the rubber boots. They paid the seller $3 each for ten pairs. She then stuffed five pairs each into two black trash bags, which they hauled back down the stairs, through the cave-like aisles and finally out into the light of the flooded streets. When they finally reached Sret, Sophy tossed her bag into the tuk-tuk as Jessica climbed in. "I have something else I need to get here. You guys go on ahead."

Sret tilted his head and gave her a doubtful smile. "Do you need help?"

"*Aut ai, Bu.* No worries, Uncle. I will be fine"

Turning back towards the market, Sophy wrapped her hair up in her *krama*, and practiced the word for underwear, "C*ao-ao draw-no-ap nuo-ai-na* Where can I get underwear?"

"Up one more floor and turn right."

On her way up the stairs, she passed a tiny stall with Hello Kitty everything. A huge plastic bag hung from the ceiling. Through the grimy plastic, she could see the Hello Kitty faces peeking out. They were mini backpacks. She stood there thinking of Sotheary's sister's ghost standing by the Mekong.

"You buy? You buy?"

"Uh-oh . . . *Awt Dtay, aw-kgoon*. No, thank you."

On the top floor, past huge bins of hair elastics and frilly satin girls' dresses in emerald, purple and yellow, she found a corner stall with stacks and stacks of bras.

"Do you have the bras with the hidden zippers in them?"

CHAPTER TWENTY

Two weeks later, Ali called again, "Sophy, can we meet? How about Jars of Clay coffee shop near the Russian Market?"

"Sure!"

They pulled up their rattan chairs at a table and ordered iced coffees.

"How was your trip to Siem Reap?" Phearun asked.

"It was fine, but I have a question for you. The karaoke on the bus?"

"You watched it?" he laughed.

"Well, the ride was too bumpy to read. Anyway, every story was utterly depressing. And the poor guy never got the girl! Never! Why does the rich guy always win?"

"Because that's the way it is. The rich are the ones with the power."

Sophy sat gazing at Phearun, expecting him to soften what he'd just said.

Ali jumped in. "Not exactly the feel-good, underdog-pulls-himself-up-against-all-odds kind of stories us westerners love, right?"

"Right."

Moving on, Ali said, "So, we — you — have stumbled upon something, the significance of which we could not have known. Normally at Lighthouse, all projects get cross-checked by a second team. But Phearun and I, well, we just cannot bring ourselves to share it with more people."

"Yes, it has been hard to read in places. Kunthea feels so . . . real, and I know she is out there somewhere, maybe very close by. I also have not shared any of it with my colleagues," Sophy sighed in agreement.

"And that is why I asked to meet. You know each time we give you a new round of entries, we have read them of course. And I want to warn you, this round is the hardest yet. Do you still want to keep going?"

Sophy rubbed her temples before replying. How could it get much worse? But she knew she could not stop now.

"I am too far in, Ali. And I have a feeling that I am somehow meant to read it. Did I tell you where I am interning?"

"I believe Phearun said, Safe Space, anti-trafficking."

"Right, and I thought I knew a lot when I arrived. And I thought, 'This will be great on my resume — such great experience.' The fact is, I am learning more from Kunthea than the internship, but I can't put that on a resume."

Ali smiled warmly, "Right then, miss Sophy Seng, let us press on!" He handed her the next set. "By the way, let us know if you have questions about anything. Of course, Kunthea does not explain what some things are, since it is her own diary, and all those things are normal to her. But they might not make sense to a foreigner."

Sophy smiled. "Thanks, I have been asking my driver lots of questions. He thinks I am just a very curious girl."

KUNTHEA'S DIARY PART FOUR

November 16, 1996
Fourteen years old

Swish swish swish. I could hear the stiff twigs of Mama's broom sweeping the dirt floor under the hut, but I would not open my eyes. The sight of my world is too much to bear. My world that used to still have some threads of sweetness, in the laughter of the little ones when they forget their hunger long enough to play. I want to sleep . . . forever. I rolled over and opened one eye. Papa's krama was on the floor by my mat. I could tie it from the rafter. The strong one in the middle. That would hold my weight. I grabbed it and draped my face. Sucking in the stench of his rice wine and grimy sweat on the cotton threads, I hid from the morning light that exposed me.

Mr. Chong's terrible words rang in my head over and over, "You will stay or get fired!" I could not drag all the bins before the bell rang. He knew all the *romoks* would be gone by the time I finished. He knew about the darkness of the road. He knew the dangers. There were three of them.

The spirits of the Mekong's dead are stirring it up. Their angry fingers churn the waters, but they disagree. Some churn it one way and some another. They want more victims to suffer with them. I could walk into it at night when everyone is sleeping and let the fingers grab me under. I could just give in to the power of the mighty Mekong, like Sotheary's sister. Would my siblings see my ghost standing on the riverbank? Would there be blood dripping down my legs? Would they know my shame?

I heard Papa's words, "Whenever you feel sad or angry, you can tell me and it will be our little secret, ok?" And the tears spilled out on either side of my face and trickled into my ears, because this is not a little secret. It is a big one, one that I cannot tell Papa — it would kill him.

The woman, she saw the blood on my legs and rushed me around the side of her house, hiding my shame, but still, sharing it. As if my pain was hers. Her sarong was still wet from bathing at her bien. Angels should be like her: not hungry for power and needing gifts. I heard her gulp and heave as she wiped my legs with her own krama. She dipped it in the bien and wrung it out and wiped again. I could hear the muffled sound of the TV from inside her house where others watched it not knowing, while she silently wiped away the dirt and blood. Hiding me in the shadows, she called in through the window bars, "I am going to Ming's house. I will be back in one hour." She took me on her own moto to a small clinic, and then paid a romok to take me home. I will never forget her.

The nurse at the clinic did not look at me. We both stared at the floor while she mumbled her instructions. She laid four pills, two pink and two yellow, in a small plastic zip-bag on the dingy metal medicine cabinet, and told me to be more careful, while the romok driver waited.

The red and white threads of the krama puffed up and then pulled in between my lips, with each heavy breath I sucked in. It is hard to hide the sound of sobbing, so it all comes out in choked breathing instead. And I thought, *This is a good place to stay; behind this veil of criss-cross threads I could still see everything: the rafters, each little dried leaf of my roof, even the rusty pins that held Mama's skirt to its thin green wire hanger and the nail it was hooked on.* But nothing could see me. If only the choking sobs would stop, and the pain in my chest that goes with trying to suppress them.

I remember when Vanna's cousin was raped. I was only about eight, but I heard the grown-ups talking. They shook their heads and whispered, "It is over for her. She will never marry now. She is ruined." Now I am ruined.

November 22, 1996
Fourteen years old

She beat her chest and muffled her sobs. "My baby girl, my baby girl?" she asked me, and I have never lied to Mama. So, I couldn't now.

It has been one week, and today I decided not to kill myself. I am ruined, but Mama and the little ones still need me. Papa, he is gone already. Swallowed up by the wine, my old Papa is gone. This new one, I do not know. If I told him, I'd see my old Papa, I know. Because he still loves me. But this time the shame is ours, not someone else's. It would break his heart, and I could not face him.

I heard the swish of Mama's broom below. She sweeps angrily these days, twice as fast. The lightened sky revealed that it must be 5:00 a.m. already, and I was ashamed for sleeping so late. I threw on my t-shirt and stretch pants and scrambled down the ladder to the bien to wash. Mama scolded me for washing too fast, "The *noom* needs to be clean, so you must be clean too." I never went back to the shoe factory, and they never sent anyone looking for me. He knew what he'd done. He knew when he made me stay, it was too dangerous. What makes people so mean and selfish? What makes them think that some people deserve to be treated like dirt? Since I was little, I heard that poor people got that way from being bad in the previous life. But now I think that maybe Da is right. He's always said, "It is not right, little one." Not right for the *barang* to have power over the poor Khmai. Not right for the rich to have power over others. Not right for evil spirits to walk right into people's bodies just because they are weak. Not right to be sent out on a dark road all alone.

So I have been making the *noom* myself and selling them, too. Sopheak has to stay in school. He is our hope. He is so smart, but every day I see the worry in his eyes as he leaves for school. His thin shoulders slump towards the road ahead, as if leaning in to the weight of all that is yet to come. This anticipation of an uncertain future hangs on us both like chains on elephants. Sometimes I wonder if he knows. I watched him until he disappeared around the bend. His poker-straight black hair sticks out and then hangs down, regardless of the wind, looking too big for his skinny frame.

Mama is different since I told her. Sometimes angry, sometimes depressed, and always weak. Like a banana tree whose fruit has gone bad, she's stopped thriving and she is letting the road dust settle onto her once-bright green leaves. And there is no rain to wash away the heavy dirt. And even if there was, this is a kind of dirt that just sticks, rain or not.

December 20, 1996
Fourteen years old

Today, I laughed. It happened when I was kneading the rice flour dough. Sela was singing a silly song with the twins. They followed her dance moves: bottoms out, arms high, jump to the left, then to the right. Just five years old and they got it! But the best part was Baby Sina. She sat naked on her mat watching and laughing so hard she fell over. Then Mama scolded Sela for not getting Sina bathed yet. And I wondered if it was ok to laugh again.

Sina is two now, so Mama is teaching again. We can buy chicken two times a week to go with the rice. But Sela had to quit school to take care of Sina and watch the twins while Mama and I work. She is so good with the kids, but she is also smart. I wish she could have stayed in school. They are so young and innocent, all of my sisters. I will never let them work in a factory. I will make sure they never walk down a dark road alone.

March 7, 1997
Fifteen years old

I stopped and turned my back to the road, pressing my krama against my face as the truck rumbled by. A cloud of fine dust enveloped me and seeped right through the worn threads of my krama. One, two three . . . fifteen counts and I can open my eyes again, breathe and walk on. One eye first — there is still a haze as the mid-day sun catches little particles of road dust floating in the air.

All is light brown. Streets, plants, houses, shoes, clothes, even the bright orange coolers for selling drinks. No rain to wash them clean. Even the thick bright green banana leaves hang low and brown. Not because they are dead. Oh, how I love to see the green return with the rains! Everything looks dead, and one simple rain brings all back to life! If only my worries could wash away with one good rain. Oh, to breathe fresh air again, to feel the after-rain breeze in my heart. Now it's as if it is dry season forever. I fear that when they do come, the rains will not clean the brown deadness from my soul this year. Not if we are still hungry, if Mama is still sick, if Papa is still drinking.

Mama has been sick again. Too sick to teach school, but she helps me make the cakes each day, and I sell until sundown. Or later if

I cannot sell it all by then. My rubber flip flop sandals are almost worn through. I hide them under the ladder under all the other sandals, so Mama will not see. I hate to hear her crying at night.

November 21, 1997
Fifteen years old

Papa took me and Sopheak to watch the boat races today! The romok stopped near the Japanese bridge. "Ok, we'll walk from here!" He looked proud. And he was sober. It had rained all night long so the river bank was muddy and Sopheak lost his flip flop in the mud. It sucked it right from his foot until the strap just tore in two. The water churned high and fast, and I remembered how Papa had taught me to swim, so long ago.

The crews called out to each other as they jumped into their boats. The sunlight was bouncing every which way. From each ripple in the water to their shiny lime green shirts and back, the colors of the crew and their beautiful boat danced on the water.

We got to see one up close, and I was so amazed at it. I ran up to touch the painted wooden side. Part of it was painted in shades of blue and white on a yellow background, in the shapes of waves, perfectly repeated. And there were bright pink lotus flower shapes with golden dots, and seven-headed Naga snakes. Each boat was a work of art. And I wondered who painted them like that and how long it took. Papa says those designs have meaning, about the greatness and power of our people, and the peace and protection of the Buddha.

Right up at the tip of the boat, tassels of a golden parasol dangled shadows over a beautiful, slim but sturdy young woman. Papa said she was the time keeper. Her silky ponytail puffed like a sail in the morning breeze, and suddenly, she was dancing! With each forward thrust, her tiny fingers bent way back into the perfect curve of the Apsara hands. She wore bright orange silk pantaloons with a white lacy fitted top, with little white beads around the neckline. The sun caught the beads each time she leaned forward in the rhythm of her dance. And with each thrust, the young men scooped the Mekong with their oars, keeping perfect time with her dance, and flying faster than any fishing boat ever could. One with its crew, each boat slid smoothly through the water as if not even trying. But when we got closer, I could see them sweating and heaving, but smiling with excitement. Some of the boats had men up front, with decorated swords, instead of the dancing girl. They swung the swords and brought them down hard on the boat bow with each stroke. I liked the ones with the girl dancer through. Before today I had only seen the races on Oam Reak's black and white TV. I never saw the bright colors dancing on the water until today.

Every year the Tonle Sap River changes directions right before the water festival. Papa says that there is a big lake up north near the famous Angkor Wat temples, called the Tonle Sap Lake. During the rainy season it swells up to six times its normal size, and when it gets too full, it pushes the water back down the river. Almost three hundred kilometers away, it meets the Mekong and the Tonle Bassac right here in Phnom Penh. So every year in November, the teams come from every province and they bring their beautiful boats with them to race.

We watched the teams race for a few hours. The pink shirts from Steung Treng Province won, but only by a few seconds. Everyone on the shore jumped and screamed until we slipped around in the mud and started laughing. Then we walked through the dense crowds looking for something to eat. Sopheak held on to Papa's shirt with one hand and reached firmly for my hand with his other hand. He has always tried to protect me, even though is younger. We reached a cart, and Papa dug into his pocket for some riel. The flames of the charcoal fire jumped about under the griddle and too close to my face. I backed away as the seller flipped three pieces of rice, bean and pork dumpling into a banana leaf bowl. The steam let me know I should hold the edges of the leaf, not underneath. I blew on it for a long time but Sopheak bit right into his. He danced about with his head cocked back and his mouth open. He should be more patient like me. Boys forget about patience when it comes to food, I think!

An hour later I saw King Sihanook! Our king is getting old, but he still loves to see his people! The Queen Mother looks taller than him now. Papa says he has shrunk shorter. Also her hairdo puffs up slightly higher than his fuzzy white hair. He had on a dark grey suit and a blue tie, just like other famous world leaders I have seen on TV. But the queen, she wore a beautiful green silk *somput* (wrap skirt), with a white lace top and a silk sash to match the skirt. Her outfits are always made from our own Cambodian silk. Every woman has a silk skirt, but only the queen has the finest of the silk made by special silkworms. They stood on the Royal Platform and bowed and blessed and greeted each boat of rowers as they passed by. Everyone was so happy, especially the rowers who got to be so close to their king! Some of them just dropped their oars in the boat and jumped and waved and bowed and danced; they were so excited. And all of them bowed in respect. I stood on my tip toes as long as I could, but the crowd was too thick, and some people were rude or maybe drunk. I was glad Papa and Sopheak were there to protect me. So we started to make our way back towards the Japanese bridge to look for a romok home. Along the way it grew dark. I heard a boom and thought it was thunder. "Look!" Sopheak called. "Fireworks!" Like giant sugar palm and coconut trees instantly growing right before our eyes, they burst forth in all the jeweled colors of wedding clothes!

I almost fell asleep on the romok. Papa caught me in his arms just like when I was a little girl on his moto.

December 19, 1997
Fifteen years old

Her eyes began to roll back in her head and I knew. Because it happens all the time now. Yelling out for Uncle Heang because Papa was not home, I slowly moved along the wall, watching her every move. The darkness was sinking down like a heavy veil, and I gasped for air. Yay started swatting at the air, and then at me. The demon voice growled from within her and I backed up against the wall, knocking the wedding picture of Mama and Papa off the wall, and the glass broke. From the corner of my eye, I saw Sina and the twins come running, with Sopheak right behind. He grabbed Sina right off the ladder just in time. She always has nightmares after the spirits possess Yay.

Her eyes were fixated on me, and I stared back, my eyes darting briefly at a reflection catching light. I caught a glimpse of a coconut cleaver just two steps away, on the table behind her, and there was nothing I could do. She stood exactly between me and the knife. Through the thumping sound of my own heartbeats, voices broke through, "It's Yay again. Come quick!" I imagined my yay standing over me, with her demon-filled eyes and supernatural strength, and the cleaver coming down ... down ... down to my head. Suddenly, they were all there: Sokleak's papa, Uncle Heang, Mr. Sok and Sotheary's oldest brother. They had her on the floor, one on each limb. I stumbled over to the ladder and leaned out. There, under the ladder, between two of the rungs, I could see my Sopheak, his long arms wrapped up tight around all the little ones, fighting tears as they hid their faces in his chest and under his arms. He looked up at me, and the desperation in his eyes pierced my heart. Sickened, I turned and looked towards Da's hut. There he sat, silhouetted in the frame of his window by the dim orange reflections off the Mekong, staring out at the powerful waters, but unmoved by the power of the spirit within Yay. His helplessness was overwhelming to me. Sometimes Da seemed so strong, and now it seemed he'd just float away on the Mekong.

July 8, 1998
Sixteen years old

I have been sleeping under Mama's net with her and Baby Sina, so I can hold her when Mama is too weak. Papa doesn't come home at night sometimes, and I cannot sleep. I imagine Papa out there in the darkness. Is he passed out on the road, where a truck will run over him? The darkness has the power to hide things, until it is too late.

August 6, 1998
Sixteen years old

I do not know what is wrong with Mama, but she is so tired. She misses school often, and we know it is just a matter of time before she will lose her job. Sopheak says the principal has been asking him about Mama. So, I had to get a factory job again. This time I used my real name, Kunthea, but Papa got my birthdate changed at the commune office. I look older now so they believed my papers at the factory.

August 9, 1998
Sixteen years old

I looked around to see if anyone else noticed. My heart was beating so loud, surely, they could hear it. I saw the Chinese writing on the gate, which reminded me of Mr. Chong at the old factory. Suddenly I grabbed the shoulder of the girl next to me because I felt sweaty and faint. At first, she pulled back, squinting her eyes at me, but when she saw my face, her eyes became soft. She offered her arm and I held on, but we did not say a word. This is a new clothing factory that is closer to home and right on the main road, so there are no long hidden roads to get there.

I am on the cutting floor. These fabrics are hard to layout for the machines because they are stretchy. We make t-shirts mostly, but fancy ones in pretty colors and prints are for girls and women, and even babies. The days are so long, but at least I am busy to pass the time, and this factory gives us a snack at 2:30 p.m. to give us more energy for working. Today we had steamed sticky rice with banana, wrapped in a banana leaf. It was cold already, but I could almost feel new energy surging through my body after just one bite. We have big fans installed into the walls also, which stirs the air and keeps us from fainting. I wonder about the girl who helped me walk on that first day, if I'd ever see her again. This factory has five thousand workers, so I think maybe not.

September 12, 1998
Sixteen years old

The rains have come but I never see it when I am working, not until I get out at the end of the day. Even though it was hard work selling the cakes, I miss being outside in the fresh air. I miss the feel of the wet dirt road under my flip flops. I miss that feeling when the white fluffy clouds gather up and hide me from the scorching sun, when the sky grows to a deep intense grey blue, when little puffs and swirls of ground dust turn into giant swoops of wind, just before the monsoon rains pour down. I miss running for cover under the little tarpaulin roofs of the shops along the road. I miss the soft roar and the blurry screened view through millions of giant drops of rain along the old dirt road I used to walk.

Today I knew it was raining though, because the air through the fans got heavy and the florescent light bulbs seemed suddenly brighter. Even though we have no windows, the sunlight usually bounces to and fro, off of the giant white metal fan blades, dimming the fake light of the bulbs in comparison. This factory is new, so the blades still look white.

Now I make twelve meurn ($30). The romok is still 2.50 even though it is not so far, because the prices have gone up due to gas prices being so high. Da says the government officials own the gas stations and they just want more money. Mama says Da should be more careful about what he says, because you never know who hears you. I know Mama is right, but in my heart, I agree with Da. I have seen the motorcades flying down the road. One black SUV after the other, full of big men who I can't see because of the darkened windows. And I wonder, is that so we can't see them? Or is it so they can't see us? Once our romok had to swerve and I almost fell off.

I have to buy my lunch at the food carts, which costs one thousand riel, twenty-five cents a day. So, all together I make $21 a month.

March 3, 1998
Sixteen years old

I found her last week during the lunch break, the girl who helped me on my first day. She was in line at the food cart with me. We got our rice and found a place to squat on our heels and eat together. Her name is Chiva. She has three younger brothers, and she had to come to the city to work and help her family. So she lives in a room with six other girls about one kilometer down the road. She pays $4 a month for the room, which is more than my romok, so she makes less than me. She saves $10 for her food for the month and sends the last $16 home.

While we were talking and eating, the wind kicked up and we both scrunched our faces shut to keep the dirt out of our eyes and mouths, but it was too late for the rice, which was suddenly reddish brown like the road. We ran to hide behind one of the carts. We scooped the dirt off the top of our rice and kept talking and eating. She looked around, and then whispered, "Guess what I got?" Digging into her jeans pocket, she pulled out a small silky piece of white cloth with big English letters: G A P. Chiva works where they sew the labels into the back pieces of the clothes before the rest of the construction.

"Why are the letters in English? I thought these garments are for the Chinese?"

Chiva said all the labels say that, and she heard that they sell the shirts in America for $25 each! Imagine that, my whole salary on one shirt! I wonder if everyone in America has enough money to spend $25 on one shirt. And I wonder why the Americans have Chinese supervisors at the factories. And I wonder if Americans would be nicer.

One time, I was sleeping at Yay and Da's hut when I was little. As I lay there next to Yay, with the moonlight dancing through the window, she started telling me about Americans bombing Cambodia. She said that was during a war, but Cambodia was not fighting America. America thought we were hiding Vietnamese soldiers in our villages so they bombed us. Yay said that some countries have more power because they have more weapons. Lots of Cambodians were killed. I am not sure if that happened before or after Pol Pot. I asked Sopheak if they learned that in school, and he said they only really studied about the Angkorian Empire in history class. He did say that Cambodia has had lots of enemies and that his teacher does not like the Vietnamese or Thais, or Americans. So, I wonder how Uncle Hak feels about living there in America? Maybe he does not know about the bombs. Yay said they were dropped from airplanes in the eastern provinces. She said there are many ponds in the east because the bombs made big holes that filled in with rainwater.

Even though this factory is better than the shoe factory, the Chinese supervisors are mean just the same. They strut through the factory, sometimes yelling and hitting someone for no reason, just to make a show of their power. Yesterday Chiva was hit. Her arm was already bruised when we met at the lunch carts. It's not right, and makes me burn with anger, like Da when he talks about the *barang*. But we cannot say anything or we will lose our jobs, or worse.

August 10, 1998
Sixteen years old

"R-A-T, H-A-T, the boy hit the rat wiss, his hat. Wat is yu name? My name is So- Pa-uk." Last night as I snuggled up with Sina on our mat under the net, as little soft beams from Sopheak's Nokia phone flashlight shone up through our bamboo floor and bounced around on the leafy roof until the battery ran out and he could not see to read. Sopheak and his friend Sochea are teaching themselves English. I have never seen anyone study so hard as my brother. Sela told me he sits there at the table with his brow furrowed and biting his lip, hunched over his school work, from 8:00 a.m. to 11:00 a.m. every day, after morning chores and sending the younger ones off to school. Then he goes to school from noon to 5:00 p.m. And when I get home at 6:00 p.m., there he sits in the hammocks with Sochea, sounding out words and quizzing each other. The back half of the house is taller off the ground than the front, since our land slopes towards the river. Sopheak is always looking for a quiet place to study or think or be alone, so he strung up some hammocks under that part of the house.

September 27, 1998
Sixteen years old

It was the first time I saw where Chiva lived. There were ten unpainted wooden doors, one about every four meters. The concrete walls were already mold infested even though it was built just one year before. The roof was almost flat, a green corrugated metal that sloped towards the front with no gutter, so there was a green slime on the walkway right under the roof edge, where the rain runs off. Each room had one red clay cooking pot outside the door. The woman was dressed nicely and wore lipstick and jewelry. "You will make a lot more money for your families and we will give you a pretty uniform to wear. All you have to do is serve beer to the customers for a few hours each night." As the girls gathered in around her, wanting to know more, I took Chiva's hand and pulled her away. "She is talking about the new karaoke bar down the road! Chiva . . . you can't! It is not just serving beer."

We agreed and she talked to her roommates more that night. Now she wants to study English. Her friend from her room told her that it is the only way to get a better job that is safe. Like me, Chiva and all the factory girls could never finish school. But I am glad for two things: Mama is a teacher, so I kept on practicing my reading long after I had to quit school, and I got to study through grade eight. I am not a good reader, but at least I know how. Chiva, and the girls in her room, not one of them studied past grade three. She said there is no use in learning to read and write Khmai. So, I am going to ask Sopheak if I can photocopy his beginner English book for Chiva. She told me today that two of the girls are moving out. They will work for the beer lady. They have to find two more girls to move in so they can afford the room.

January 19, 2000
Eighteen years old

Papa is sick. The doctor says he has the sweet urine disease. He only eats rice and drinks palm wine, but somehow his belly gets fatter. He lost his job at the police station, because he was always drunk or sick or both. So now there is no money. Mama cannot teach at the school. She is too weak. Sometimes when Papa does come home, Mama cries and hits him, but he never hits her back. He just stares out the window. All my life I have watched them, the people I love so much. Life gets too hard and they start staring out the window. No tears, no talking, just staring.

CHAPTER TWENTY-ONE

Sophy

The monks were chanting in Sophy's dream when suddenly she awoke with a flash of light and a clap of thunder. The loudest she'd ever heard, it seemed to shake the building, and she found herself wondering if it might be something else, like a gunshot. Jumping from her bed, she headed for her bedroom door and yanked it open. Jessica was already running down the hall screaming when another flash of light illuminated her slipping and falling. Sophy reached out to help but it was too late. They were both on the tile floor, and realized it was covered with water. A low rumble was escalating to a loud roar as the monsoon rain poured buckets on their roof and rattled the windows.

"Are you ok?" Sophy grabbed Jessica by the shoulders.

"I think so!" she yelled over the roar, while rubbing her hip.

"It's rainwater in the house. Get some towels!"

Afraid of anything electric while standing in the flooded room, she opted to not turn on a lamp and made her way gingerly to the balcony door. A small river was flowing in under the metal door. Sophy leaned in with all her weight and pushed the door open against the wind. It slammed against the outdoor wall. The balcony was filling up like a swimming pool, as she thought the drain must be plugged.

While Jessica threw their towels all over the floor, Sophy got down on her hands and knees and crawled through the rising water to the drain. Shoving one hand into the simple hole in the side of the balcony ledge, she realized it wasn't blocked at all. It was simply too small for this torrent. Jessica appeared in the doorway, spitting the rain away from her face, each blonde curl channelling water like mini waterslides. She handed Sophy a plastic bowl and they both began to bail.

Thirty minutes later, soaked through and exhausted, they shivered in the kitchen. "I thought it was a gunshot," Jessica confessed.

"Don't feel bad, Jessica. So did I."

Glancing at the clock, which read 3:30, Jessica yawned, "We're gonna be sore tomorrow."

"Right, because we have never had a wrestling match with a monsoon rain before. We'd better get in shape."

Jessica sighed and laughed out loud.

Sophy gazed at the sturdy concrete walls of their kitchen. *I'm just glad we have more than one wall.* And she wondered if Kunthea still lived in the one-walled hut. She imagined the same storm pummelling her family as they huddled together against the one wall.

As they headed for dry clothes in their rooms, a new sound rose above the steady rain. It was monks chanting.

"It's only 3:30?" Jessica wondered.

A funeral. Sophy remembered the diary. The funeral started when a person died. She had not been dreaming before the storm woke her. They really were chanting.

"Somebody died."

Leaning over the rattan couch and peering out the front window, they could see blurry figures moving about under one florescent bulb, right across the street. And there, on a wooden table lay the body.

"You see that guy? He's dead."

"Oh my God, Sophy! You're freaking me out! How do you know that? Maybe he is just sleeping!"

"I . . . I read about it. They call the monks right away because they are scared about the spirit of the dead person. I heard the chanting before the storm."

The chanting grew louder and louder. "No sleeping for us," Sophy lamented. Raising her own voice to be heard, "The chants from the *wat* are loud, but this is bone-rattling loud."

"Not sure I could sleep anyway," Jessica yelled. "There is a dead person lying on a table across the street." She rolled her eyes and fell back on the couch. "What next?"

As soon as it was light, they ventured out to find a noodle shop for breakfast, as far from the loudspeakers as possible.

"*Dti Nih, Dti Nih!* Go through here!" The guard motioned towards the funeral tent.

Between 3:30 and 5:30 a.m., they had managed to erect a funeral tent, and it completely blocked the street, right up to each gate on both sides of the narrow road. Sophy walked the Chaly quietly through the tent, with Jessica carrying their helmets close behind. Scrappy teenage workers in jeans and flip flops wrapped metal tent poles in long shiny pieces of black and white cloth. Others pushed round metal folding tables into place and covered them with stained white satin.

Making her way to the road outside the tent, she spotted a gold framed portrait on a wooden stool. Tendrils of black smoke twirled upward form dirty little terra-cotta pots, each over-stuffed with burning incense sticks, on either side of the portrait. Blinking the sting of the smoke away, she looked back at the portrait. He was young. Maybe twenty. *Was it an accident?* Her focused shifted. Inches behind the photo and the pots were two white shapes — feet, under a shroud of white gauze. The body was right there.

Sophy took a deep breath and proceeded to the edge of the tent to leave. Mounting the Chaly and glancing back one more time, she saw in the shadows by the body a woman bent over in continuous bow, her head almost to the floor. On the other side of the draped body, three monks chanted into microphones.

CHAPTER TWENTY-TWO

It was another Saturday night in Phnom Penh, and friends were hanging out at Matthias' flat near the Wat Botum Park.

Matthias was expounding the virtues of some favorite books on ending poverty.

"I am telling you, it is a matter of awareness. Poverty is solvable. Rich countries just need to recognize their moral obligation, which in the end makes a better world for us all. If wealth was only distributed, there would be no hungry people. And it is really — what is it you say in English — a winning thing?"

"A win-win," Sophy and Jessica chimed in unison.

Matthias paced when he was discussing anything important.

"Sounds pretty optimistic, Matthias. What do you think, Sophy?" Thomas was curious as to whether Sophy's heritage might impact her thinking.

"I am not sure. I am just wondering if it might be more complex than all that. I mean, I am no expert. "

Her mind drifted to the diary. The thoughts of a five-year-old Khmai girl were already challenging her in ways she could not articulate, even to herself. On the surface it was just a diary of young child. But children are so . . . honest. She thought about the entry on the French colonization: "Back when the *barang* were in charge of Cambodia."

"On one hand, I have always thought that education equalled progress. Moving towards a better world. But Pol Pot was educated."

Thomas laughed, "And insane!"

Sophy went on, "Maybe. He thought he could wipe out greed by wiping out the elite, the educated class. But I'm thinking . . . who gets to decide who the greedy are? Where do you draw that line?"

Jessica continued the thought, "It is like he was playing God."

"Yeah, I guess so," Sophy contemplated.

"And by the way, the French didn't do this country much good either."

"Except for . . ." Thomas began and they all chimed in, "Baguettes, cheese and beautiful buildings!"

Sophy wanted to ask her friends what they thought of the spiritual beliefs: stuff about demon possession and the fears of the people. But she couldn't do it. They'd think she was crazy. And she was determined to protect her secret and Kunthea's privacy. But the questions burned into her soul at times. Lost in her thoughts, she nodded to herself, *I will ask Sret and Phearun about all that.*

Seeing her nodding to no one, Matthias gave her a funny look.

Ugh, he already thinks I am crazy!

CHAPTER TWENTY-THREE

"Sret, what is the word for cow's hump?"

"Bo-kgo, spelled bokor in English."

"What, you mean like the Caltex where Kem Ley was shot? It means the cow's hump Caltex?"

He laughed. "Yes, but it is just the name of that area. There is also a mountain named that in Kampot Province down at the edge of the ocean."

"I heard about that. Did the French build a palace there?"

"Well, it was a casino and hotel actually . . . and a French church so people could go there after gambling and make offerings."

Sophy continued, "So what about the word *barang*?"

"Well, it actually means the French, but many people use it to mean 'foreigner.'"

"Sophy *chgnol r'hoat*! Wonders continuously," Sret laughed. "Sophy has many questions!"

Rumors that some former traffickers were actively looking for a few of their girls meant longer trips that ventured way off the path to the safehouse. Sret pulled into a narrow drive and slowed. Straight ahead, she saw that this path seemed to lead straight into a river. Having built trust in Sret, Sophy waited to see his plan.

"*Bi-neac, muey moto.* Two people, one moto." A teenage girl sat on a wooden table under the shade of some trees, while a toddler played next to her. She picked pieces of jellied sticky rice with coconut and yellow bean off a banana leaf and handed them to the child, who grinned with delight in anticipation of each bite. A basket of loose riel notes sat by her side.

"*Bi-bo-an.* Two thousand riel."

"*Awgkoon, bu.* Thank you, Uncle." She took the money, and Sret slowly descended the hill towards the river, just as a rickety wooden ferry pulled up to the floating dock. The ferry driver leaned his weight against a rope, closing the gap between dock and ferry as Sret heaved the bike forward onto the boat. Sophy climbed off the bike and took off her helmet. The morning sun danced on the water. Turning her face towards the wind, she saw at least six fishing boats, some so close you could almost touch them. A young mother held a naked baby over the edge of a boat and dipped him into the water. He cooed as she pulled him back to her lap and wrapped him in a *krama*. A muscular young man stood at the back, peering out at the river ahead, leaning into the long end of a wooden rudder. At the helm stood a thin but also muscular man with greying hair. Missing a leg, he leaned on the oar with his weight. A piled mass of fishing net lay by his one foot.

Uncle Heang, is that you? Sophy's heart skipped beat.

CHAPTER TWENTY-FOUR

At 4:00 p.m., Matthias and Ra, his Khmai work partner, limped into the office, all scraped up.

"We were chased by a crazy bull!" Matthias explained while they got out the first aid kit to clean the guys up.

Just when Sophy was giving Matthias a proper I-don't-believe-you look, Ra chimed in.

"Sorry *bong*, brother. When you drive the shortcut, I did not see cows, so I am thinking, no problem, we are safe. The bull cow always hate that sound of that CRM, and they chase it. It hurts their ears."

"It's ok, Ra. Not your fault. Now I know."

Safe Space had kept that Honda CRM two-stroke bike for interns exactly like Matthias. The mopeds were too small for a guy over six feet tall. Matthias liked the bike, except for the fact that it was a kick start. "Just starting that bike works up a sweat that soaks my clothes before I go anywhere!"

Just then, Sophy's phone rang. "Hey, we have fourteen more entries." Ali asked if she could come in on her way home.

KUNTHEA'S DIARY PART FIVE

February 8, 2000
Eighteen years old

She always wears a krama scarf, but not like the rest of us. Hers is wrapped around her head like the Cham women, but then across her face too. Sometimes she smiles at me from behind the krama threads, and her eyes are beautiful when she smiles. They do not let her keep the krama over her face like that at the factory, so we all know about her acid-burned face. It is mostly on her right side, and sometimes I wonder how it happened. Was she the wife or the mistress? Was she sleeping? Did she love the man, or was he just using her? She always gets off the romok at Sway Pak, before we cross the ferry to the east side of the Mekong where my village is. There are always foreign men there walking in and out of the Sway Pak road. I heard there are brothels there with very young girls that the foreign men like. It turns my stomach when I see the men. Sometimes I imagine myself leaping from the romok and attacking them. One time I dreamt that I had them all handcuffed and lined up. I was boldly pacing along the row, staring at each one with a power in my eyes so intense, they just began to fall. At the end of the row, three of them were Khmai, teenagers whose faces I knew. They saw me coming and screamed in terror. They tried to run, but I tripped the first one and they took turns falling. Then I woke up, completely soaked with sweat. I thought the power in the dream should make me feel better, but it did not.

Someday I will ask her name, the girl with the beautiful eyes. Maybe we can be friends.

March 1, 2000
Eighteen years old

It has been six years since the fire and four years since I decided not to kill myself. Yay gets the spirits at least two times a week now. Papa is sick, and Mama is tired. Sopheak and me, we try to manage.

July 2, 2000
Eighteen years old

This time, I cannot hide from death. This is not Sotheary's sister, or Vannara's da. It is my papa. They called me at the factory to say it was the end. I spent all I had on the moto taxi home. The tears were sticking to my dirty face and the road dust stuck to my tears. I kept gulping and sucking air through sobs, as the moto bounced down the road. They stood along the road, my neighbors watching me with pity in their eyes. I jumped off the moto and numbly ran between the concrete walls of the tiny alley. At first, I thought the walls would fall in on me, and then they were gone . . . I could not see on either side. Just straight ahead. Just like during the fire, the path before me was a tunnel. I climbed our too-short ladder and fell at his side on my knees. I ran my fingers along the soft ridges of the faded mat, trying to push death away. His heavy head fell towards me. He caught my gaze and whispered, "Kunthea . . . Papa loves you." For a moment I saw him, my old Papa. In that moment, the reflection in his weak eyes danced and I saw all the life we'd shared. The secrets we shared. And the one we did not. In that moment I was glad he never knew what happened to me. I lay my head on his chest, gently, and then I saw him smile just a little. One wisp of a moment later, he was gone. Papa took his very last breath and I wanted to take my last too. But my lungs kept on breathing against my will.

July 3, 2000
Eighteen years old

Death is here. It is right there laid out on the family table, next to our house. It is right there lurking inside Papa's stiff body. It is right there in the fearful dance of the monks' chants. The incense and manipulations of spirits have come and gone, and back again to haunt. But I am not afraid. Death has grabbed my papa and crumpled him up, but his spirit will never bring me harm. I felt angry with the monks for thinking so. They do not know my papa. He tried to drink his sorrow away, but he never hurt us, and he never will.

Aunt Mony and Uncle Heang helped Yay and Da prepare his body and we all helped lift him onto a clean mat. Uncle Reak brought the picture of Papa in his police uniform. Sotheary's papa brought us a beautiful golden frame. Papa looked so strong in that photo, especially in that golden frame. Sopheak and I tried to wash two tin cans for the incense, but I felt ashamed of them. Mama kept wiping the glass that lay over his portrait. She would gaze at it and then find another smudge and rub harder, as if searching for who he used to be.

The music started at 4:00 p.m., and then they started coming: policemen and teachers and every seller in the market, the fishermen and their families. They all remembered the old strong, honest Papa, who had cared for them. They remembered that he was there, through weddings and babies, their fights and the fire. They chose to remember this Papa, and I was proud of him again.

The monks came and they chanted. *O-o-o-a-n-d-a-a-w-w-n-n-a-b-o-o-d-h-a-pub-a-a-I-idt.* Blasting over the speaker horn, the nasal monotone sound rung in my ears, and I prayed to Buddha that the chants were carrying Papa to a safe place.

Kneeling there on the floor in her funeral skirt, with only her clasped hands between her face and the floor, Mama bowed in continuous respect. But I could see her shoulders shaking with each sob. Was she remembering the husband of her youth? Before she learned to love him? Or the one she grew to love, after I was born? Surely, she chose to forget the husband who drank himself to death. The eerie chants mean something, but nothing to me. What good is a high royal spirit language if we cannot understand it? Papa is gone and that makes no sense either. Summoned by the monks' sickly chants, the spirits gathered over our one walled hut, mocking us. Ancestors and demons, but no good angels. And not Papa. He was gone for sure, and my heart sank deep into my soul where it could not even breathe.

July 8, 2000
Eighteen years old

Sokaa kicked the tallest wooden stilt on the slope side of the house, and it shook the house. He was angry all the time since Papa died. Mama pulled herself up by the window bars to see, and then dropped back to her mat, sobbing. None of us tried to stop him. This is how it feels, when death robs your own family. It is a whole different kind of pain. You can't breathe. I never knew that the others couldn't breathe.

When Papa was drinking, I lied to myself that we were still safe. But now he is gone, and I know we are not.

September 28, 2000
Eighteen years old

The rain wouldn't stop, but I kept on moving, slipping into the muddy holes. I didn't even care about my holiday skirt soaking up the muddy waters. Yay held a dim flashlight she borrowed from Mr. Hong, and I carried the tin buckets full of sticky rice balls. Others were moving quietly down the road as well, past the dark empty market, and up to the high road. I could see their silhouettes and shadows in the misty rain, funneling in through the temple gateway. All were there for the same reason: to feed the hungry ghosts of their dead. Yay said we had to go at least seven times during the fifteen days. Because Papa had been dead for almost three months and he would be so hungry. In my heart I do not believe that Papa was so bad that he is in the deepest hell. But what if Yay is right? What if Papa is there and he is hungry? How can I not go? I threw the rice balls in all eight directions, and Yay made me do it twice, because of her aunt Sophea who haunts us every week. We got back home at 4:00 a.m. and I lay on my mat until dawn. But I did not sleep. I wondered how hungry Papa would be next year, after a full twelve months plus three. Tomorrow night, Sopheak will go with Yay.

March 2, 2002
Twenty years old

"Be careful, *bong srey*, older sister." It just all seems so . . . so dangerous." Sopheak cringed and held his head in his hands. I was excited to tell Sopheak and Sochea all I had learned, but he shushed me until we could find a safe place. We climbed the tall ladder of Sochea's hut, down closer to the Mekong, and I told them everything. "For our salary we are supposed to work eight hours a day, six days a week, not twelve hours or seven days, and if we do we should be paid overtime. They cannot hit us. We get real bathroom breaks, and the toilets have to work properly. They have to run the fans so we do not faint from the heat."

And I told them about our Union President, Chea Vichea. So fearless he is! So far he was wounded in the grenade attack of 1997, and he was beaten by armed guards at the Thai Ya garment factory for passing out leaflets to workers about their rights. They sat listening as I paced with excitement in the small darkened hut. Sopheak is right. It is dangerous. But for the first time in a long time, I feel powerful.

All my life, I heard about power but never felt it before. Others were powerful, the French *barang*, the rich, and the demons. Not me. Not my family. I stopped talking and looked at my brother, wanting him to feel it too. He winced at me and shook his head. He'd been doing his part, studying hard. He hadn't known my life at the factory, and that made me sad. Not because factory life is good, but because we have big parts of our lives that the other one is not part of. And I longed for the days when we were young, when we played on the boats and ran through the market, when we had the eyes of children and we couldn't see what lay ahead.

The light was fading and the boats knocked each other softly. Mosquitoes buzzed in and out of the window bars. I looked around at Sochea's hut. It was even smaller than ours. The stilts are higher because it is closer to the Mekong. And I knew in my heart, that this power I felt could still never stop the Mekong from flooding, or the darkness from closing in.

April 8, 2002
Twenty years old

When Chea Vichea finished speaking, I glanced at my friend Roath next to me, and for a moment our eyes bugged out in amazement. I felt thrilled and scared and excited all at once. His face is square and his eyebrows are dark and thick, which somehow makes him seem like a big man when he is not. In fact, he is a bit thin, like my Sopheak. Perhaps he also does not have enough to eat. While he taught us, his younger brother sat in the chair next to him and nodded along, and I could see that he was standing strong with his brother.

It has been one month since I passed the last interview. "Why do you want to be a leader? Can you read and write?"

They liked my answers, and I was chosen. There are five thousand workers in my factory, and now there are five of us to lead them, one for every thousand. Roath covers the east wing of our floor, and I have the west wing. There is a political leader who believes that factory workers should be given better wages, and that we should not suffer abuse. I am a worker, but now I have authority to watch the Chinese supervisors. If they hit, I can report them. And I am not afraid.

The Free Trade Union of Workers in the Kingdom of Cambodia — that is our organization. And our leader believes in us. Just because we had to quit school doesn't mean we are not smart. They made a deal with the factory owners, that us leaders could have one day off for a conference to study.

So, there I was, with forty others, a notebook in hand, writing as fast as I could, and remembering *Necru* Sophia's plea, "You're so smart, Kunthea. You must stay in school!" And I hoped she'd be proud to see me on this day.

"Although it is not often followed, there is a labor law in Cambodia. If you are to lead in your factories, you need to know these laws. You are the ones who can hold your supervisors and managers accountable. You can remind them of the responsibilities they have."

It was a very long day and although my head was overflowing with new information, I was somehow energized.

Since the training, we were given arm band badges to wear at the factory, along with Nokia cell phones, which were all topped up with money, and the number of the local police already in the contacts.

Off-kilter, the single wall-mounted fan clicked loudly every time it rotated towards me and Roath, and then sucked in the torn dirty-yellow window curtain on the return swing. A young man reached up and held the curtain down, so that no one could peer in from the alleyway outside. The air hung heavy and I wiped my neck with my krama. The April heat was stifling, but his words were like fresh breeze. "Dare to express yourselves. Have no fear. Strength lies in unity."

There were eighteen of us, from six different factories, on the floor with our backs pressed against the cement walls of Chea Vichea's simple house. His little girl sat in her mama's lap and played with the fabric folds of her green sarong skirt until she drifted off to sleep. Gently laying her on the woven grass mat, her mama slipped off her Hello Kitty rubber pink shoes. Watching her little black ponytail fall back from her perfect tiny and peaceful face, I was overcome with a sudden sadness. I got lost in thinking about that night so long ago that left me ruined. No man will ever want me as a wife, and I will never have children of my own. Shaking off the sadness, I refocused on Vichea and the better life we could make for all the children, for my siblings and their future children.

April 28, 2002
Twenty years old

On the first of May, we are planning to march on to the Ministry of Labor and Social Affairs and then the Municipal Courthouse. Although we can legally provide accountability now, there are still many issues. What is legal and what really happens are two different things. One by one, people shared their own experiences:

"We were promised bonuses for meeting target production. We met the targets but were never paid. That was five months ago."

"I was offered a bribe to resign. They do not want our kind around."

"The government labor inspectors came last week. They were in and out in five minutes, with pockets bulging and smiling faces."

October 22, 2003
Twenty-one years old

At dinner tonight, I read the paper out loud.

"Scenes of unfettered grief engulfed mourners in the corridors of the Preah Sihanouk Hospital on Tuesday as doctors fought to save the life of popular singer Touch Srey Nich, 24, who was shot twice in the face and once in the neck by assailants in a daytime attack that left her mother dead . . . The singer had also recorded a collection of songs in support of the Kampuchea Krom community in Vietnam's south. The songs deal with such themes as corruption, border issues and the suffering of the Kampuchea Krom in Viet nam." According to witnesses, the singer was gunned down as she left a flower shop on Monireth Boulevard; her mother and younger brother were waiting outside in a vehicle. When the gunman began firing, the singer's mother jumped from the vehicle and ran towards her daughter. Firing his last round into the star's head as she slumped to the ground, the hit man raised his weapon and shot her mother once, witnesses said.

Yay leaned towards me in a hushed but stern tone, "Kunthea! We lived through Pol Pot. *This* is small thing. Do you understand me? You must be careful."

Mama taught me to read, and read I will! I will not be like the countryside people who believe what they are told, who cannot read it for themselves. It has happened at least once and sometimes twice a month for the last eight months. Those who dare to stand up are shot. This is the second shooting this week. Opposition radio reporter Chuor Chetharith was killed on Saturday, and today this. I want to be brave, like Vichea, but I am not sure I know how. I just feel angry all the time.

November 9, 2003
Twenty-one years old

"You've been so caught up in the Union, *bong*," Sopheak reminded me last night, of that time when Papa took us to see the boat races.

"You are fighting for a better future, and that is good, but what about today? Will they have good memories along the path, like we do? I have saved a little money for the food carts and romo*k*."

He reached into his pocket and pulled out some riel. "The boat races end today. Let's take them."

He was right. Sela, Sokaa, the twins and Sina had never been to see the races. Like us, before Papa took us, they'd only seen it on the black and white TV. It was the colors that surprised me so much when we went with Papa. Sela is eighteen now and Sokaa is sixteen. Sela has always enjoyed the little ones, and today was no different. She danced and jumped with Sina (who is nine now) when they saw the bright boats flying through the waters and the dancing girl up front. But the best memory from today for me was watching Sokaa when he popped a hot pork bun in his mouth too soon, just like Sopheak did six years ago. He pranced around with his mouth half open. Mony and Malia laughed at him until they fell down on the slippery river bank, and Sokaa laughed at himself too.

January 22, 2004
Twenty-two years old

The road dust was sticking to my teary face. Roath leaned over the handlebars of her parked moto and buried her face in her arms. I straddled the seat behind her and leaned my head on her back for a long moment. "We have to go in, oan." She blew her nose into her krama. I took my own krama, brushed her hair out of her face and tried to dab it dry but her tears just kept dropping. We held hands and moved into the crowd. I pressed forward, through the wailing, the cameras, pulling Roath behind me.

Chea Vichea is dead. Two men just drove up to the newsstand by Wat Langka and shot him twice at 9:00 a.m. this morning. He was reading the newspaper there, like he did every morning. His brother started the phone chain, and we all knew within the hour. They tried to keep us away but we showed our Union Leader badges. His widow sat hunched over his body, which was not yet covered by the gauze. We could see the wound to his head, but his chest was covered. I was strong for Roath, but as she sobbed into my shirt, I wondered what we'd do without our leader.

January 26, 2004
Twenty-two years old

Today the police announced they'd caught the killers. But we all knew they didn't do it. I was at Oam Reak's noodle shop and the TV news was praising the police chief for work well done. Sok Sam Oeun and Born Samnang. Two innocent men who will confess, because they have to.

On Sunday we honored him along with thousands of others. His casket was old, but they repainted it. Dead or alive, rich or poor, they cannot take away his honor.

September 5, 2004
Twenty-two years old

Holding Sina to my chest so she could not see, I watched the little red clock. It had already been thirty minutes. The men took turns holding her and resting. The spirit has moved, from Yay to Mama. It happens two to three times a week now, and I cannot keep up. It makes her grab knives. It makes her scream. It finds power where there is none, there in Mama's small weak body. I am afraid it will kill her. One of these times, she just won't wake up afterwards. Then we will be true orphans.

The girls are afraid to sleep in the hut now. So, I saved ten *mearn*, $25, and went to see the spirit teller. He said this is a special spirit that needs offerings of meat. I bought a pig's hind leg. The seller at the market chopped it from the bloody animal. When I laid it on the plate, it looked exactly like the pig's legs at the morning wedding call.

And I wondered how a groom's gift and a demon's food could be one and the same.

Sopheak and I walked to the temple. He carried the plate and some incense he had bought. Aunt Mony had given us a good vase for the incense, so we took the meat and all of it to the monks. We each lit the incense sticks until they were all gone and my eyes burned from the smoke. With every bow, we tried to wretch that spirit away from Mama, over and over and over. The monks' rhythmic chants raised in unison, as a powerful echo over each grassy roof to our own little one walled hut. When we returned home, Mama lay sleeping peacefully.

But it was back in just two days. I do not have $25 every two days. I think we will all die.

CHAPTER TWENTY-FIVE

Sophy

"You're a strange one, Sophy Seng. Always somehow staring off into space. I would be glad to know your thoughts at times." A few friends had invited Sophy to watch the Water Festival. After reading about it from Kunthea's perspective, she was super curious. Overall, she had been pretty reclusive, obsessed with her secret reading. The whole situation had her inside her head way too much, and the lack of social outlet was probably a bad thing, she thought. So, she'd said yes.

The races took place right across from the Royal Palace grounds, and the finish line was at the gazebo, just as described by Kunthea nineteen years prior! However, the king had died in 2012, and his son, King Sihamoni, had taken his place watching the races. Sophy had the impression this king was not so revered as his father had been.

The group had rented two hotel rooms with balconies, right above the street. From there they could watch the races without fighting the crowds. The city swells to four times its normal population for the three-day festival, with villagers from every province camping out in any nook they can find. In fact, this was the second year the races were back on, after a tragedy several years back, in 2010. Over 350 people had died on a suspension bridge in a human stampede. The cause for the panic was hotly debated and blame was thrown around, but in the end, they had to tear the bridge down because no one dared use it for fear of all the ghosts.

Matthias was right. Sophy's thoughts were far away, on the Water Festival of 1997. She was seeing the whole scene through the eyes of Kunthea, pondering the slow demise of her father, and how this day had reminded Kunthea of the father he'd been and, it seemed, the father he wanted to be.

From their spot above the crowded street and the river, the aromas of fried bananas and steamed pork buns became too much to resist, so the crew headed out in search of the local culinary delights. Matthias was walking closely behind Sophy. At 6'2", he stood well above all the local people, and even Sophy, who was tall for a Cambodian woman. So, he was able to see that a group of Khmai youth were surrounding them, and beginning to close in. Their eyes darted at each other as they swelled inward like a swarm of bees, and it was clear to Matthias that they had a plan. Instinctively, he pushed in closer to Sophy and circled his arms around her for protection. He pushed out with all the resistance his arm muscles could muster, and then realized that he could not have lowered his arms if he'd tried. They were stuck. Pressed in place around Sophy, while he felt hands reaching in all four of his jean pockets. And suddenly they had vanished. It was the first time Sophy felt truly fearful since she'd arrived in Cambodia. The pressure was suffocating, and she could only think of those 350 people who had been trampled. She shook her head as the moment passed. Matthias grabbed her hand firmly and headed back towards the hotel balcony stairs. It was not until they were all reunited back upstairs that he shared that his wallet and phone had been stolen.

"So sorry, Matthias," Jessica empathised.

"It's ok. They are desperate. I wonder what I'd do in their shoes," Matthias sympathized, and Sophy was impressed that he did not seem angry.

"Yeah, but how do we know? Maybe they blow the money on drugs?" Thomas wondered.

Sophy listened, thinking of Kunthea and her family. "That's always possible, but I agree with Matthias. I think mostly they are desperate."

Jessica went on, "It is more complicated than I thought before. There are a lot of NGOs here, doing development work, but I wonder about what is actually effective."

"Educational ones," Thomas replied. "When they understand that they can grow and learn, they will begin to succeed. Isn't that how our countries developed, schools and universities?"

Sophy silently wondered what it would mean to "understand that you can grow and learn" versus actually believing it, when everything in your life says otherwise and has since you were born.

Jessica responded, "Yeah, but does education alone change mindset? I remember watching a reporter on TV during the Iraq war, when I was a kid. He said something like, 'What if they do not want democracy?' I thought, 'Who wouldn't want freedom and justice?' But maybe those things are luxuries. I am beginning to think that Cambodians just want to maintain the status quo."

"You mean like *just keep the peace*?" Matthias asked.

"Yeah, especially the older ones, over forty, because they remember war."

All of them fell silent then, and they watched the scene below. This crowd was young, a generation whose parents won't talk. A generation that did not understand what their parents went through. Sophy bit her lip and turned her face away from her friends as she gulped back tears. *It is for generations like these that monuments are built.* Sophy remembered traveling to Washington, D.C., with her high school US government class. They had stopped in Harrisburg, Pennsylvania, on the way. There was a monument there to those who died in the holocaust. It was titled, "Never Again." The inscription called for educating future generations, so they'd not forget and never allow such atrocities to happen again. And back then, Sophy had believed that could happen. But now, she couldn't help but think, *It happened again in 1975 in Cambodia*, and it was still happening today.

CHAPTER TWENTY-SIX

Bethany sat behind her desk, a smirk on her face, "Sophy, these girls have enough problems without you reminding them of all the primitive superstitions they have."

Sophy had been asking the girls questions, about what they believed, about what they had seen, about their fears. And she had been working hard on not acting so American. She had studied their mannerisms and realized that overall Cambodians were much more polite. She learned to do the *somphea* (bowing with her hands together) when she greeted people. During group sharing, she'd started sitting on the floor with her legs to one side, which actually hurt. The girls were relieved that she could understand their language, and some of them had begun to open up with her. It drove Bethany crazy when Sophy was able to respond without translation, as if Sophy was intentionally trying to one-up her when in fact she'd just understood and got caught up in the discussion.

Bethany went on, "All that stuff just keeps them from moving forward."

Exactly, thought Sophy. *And what if it is not just superstition? What if . . . it is . . . real?*

"Just stick to your job, Sophy. Don't mess with their heads."

Bethany had seemed threatened by Sophy from day one. And she did not seem interested in discussion — she already knew it all. Sophy wasn't trying to give her a hard time. She decided to steer clear of Bethany, while she continued to seek answers. Kunthea wouldn't let her do otherwise.

CHAPTER TWENTY-SEVEN

Sophy and Sret had passed these factories before, but never at shift change. Hundreds of girls swarmed outside the gate. They all wore headscarves made from exactly the same knit fabric: light blue with little white flowers. She was glad for the crowd so that Sret had to move slowly through, because she wanted to see them. She wanted to hear their voices and breathe the air they breathed. She wanted to see inside their bowls of rice. She wanted to walk with them, arm in arm, and protect them from harm.

One kilometer down the road, more girls were filing in and out of a dingy alley with rows of rooms on either side, like the one where Chiva lived. Sophy strained to see their eyes, their faces, to see who they really are, not what they'd become. She wanted to tell Sret to stop, but he was really beginning to wonder about her and all her questions.

One week later, Sophy picked up the next nineteen entries from Phearun.

KUNTHEA'S DIARY PART SIX

October 10, 2004
Twenty-two years old

Reaching the riverfront, I sank down on the granite ledge. I do not know when I started walking. I do not know when my foot started to bleed from the rubbing of my sandal. I did not even notice or care. But I knew it was seven kilometers from my village to the riverfront. I just had to leave so I could try to think. Possessed by the fears racing through my head, I tried to squeeze them out with my fingers. What if the twins start to die for lack of food? How will I watch it? What if Sopheak got sick and could not help me? What will I do when the lenders come to take the house? Is it better to starve, or to watch your mama disappear into the clutches of demons? Shall I watch them use Mama's own arms to swing a knife, slashing the very flesh she gave birth to? The arms that held us, that rocked us to sleep?

How will I know when the little ones are going to die? Will they stare at me with big hollow eyes and just stop breathing, or gasp for air? It is too much. I cannot bear the thought of it.

"Are you ok, *b'oan srey*, younger *sister*?" His voice was kind enough, but not welcome.

Squinting up at his sun-silhouetted figure, I wiped my teary, dirty face with my krama, and turned away. "I'll be fine."

So, he quietly sat there next to me and we both said nothing for a very long time, I think. My mind drifted back into visions of despair, of starving, dying children and my mama consumed by the evil spirit, until my head was aching and I could barely breathe. And

I remembered not breathing like that when Papa died and I felt death looming over me again.

"Can I tell you a story?" His words jolted me from the grip of my own despairing thoughts.

He wore silver-wire-framed glasses that kept sliding down on his nose. He'd alternate pushing the glasses back up with one hand and wiping his sweat with a krama in his other hand. He looked to be about mid-forties, thin with baggy grey dress pants and worn black leather shoes.

I was irritated at his presence. "Where did you come from? Do you work around here?"

"I am a shoe maker. I come here sometimes to read and watch the boats . . . and to pray." He held a black leather-bound book, quite worn, that said "*Preah Gom-bee*" on the front. He pushed his glasses up on his nose again, so that they clearly framed his eyes. They reminded me of Papa's eyes, and I turned away again.

"No, stories have no power. Just like gods and monks and spirit tellers, no real power."

My mind was sucked back into those repeating thoughts. Stories are just tales. They cannot stop the pain in our stomachs. They cannot pay back my debts. But I did not tell him that. He was a stranger, even though his eyes were kind.

He spoke of the god named Preah Jesu.

"They are all powerless, just like me. And I do not need a foreign god."

"What if I told you that Preah Jesu has power, even over evil spirits?"

"I wouldn't believe you."

Hoping he would leave, I looked away from him, out at the river and the row of docked boats along the muddy bank. A dirt-smudged boy with lice-filled hair approached me with his jasmine worship trinkets for sale. I shook my head and the fragrance floated past my face and out to the Mekong. This same Mekong of my village so far down the road. The same Mekong that almost swept Uncle Heang away before Papa saved him. The Mekong that stole Sotheary's sister from her house and left her and her Hello Kitty backpack ghost roaming my village forever. The Mekong I should have walked into and ended it all.

A scrappy teenage boy trotted down the bank, coaxing his band of foreign tourists out towards his double-decked wooden cruise boat. "Little more! See . . . dry here . . . wood for you! No mud!" A woman in a white flowing skirt tip toed along fretfully, while another man fussed over her.

All the while the man waited quietly and said nothing, but he also didn't leave.

I turned and looked at him. He was about the age that Papa would be now. And his black eyes burned into me with kindness.

"What does Preah Jesu want from me to make the evil spirit leave my Mama? I have no money left, so best to forget about it."

"Nothing."

I laughed.

He went on to explain. "There is no offering you can make to have this power. You need only to believe and become a *Suh r'boh Preah*, a student of Preah Jesu. This power comes from Him and there is nothing you can give in return."

He showed me words in his book, a book he called Preah Buntuel (The Words of God). I reached for the book and began reading the words for myself.

"*God saved you by his grace when you believed. And you can't take credit for this; it is a gift from God. Salvation is not a reward for the good things we have done, so none of us can boast about it*[1]."

"*I pray that your hearts will be flooded with light so that you can understand the confident hope he has given to those he called—his holy people who are his rich and glorious inheritance.*[2]"

"*One day Jesus called together his twelve disciples and gave them power and authority to cast out all demons and to heal all diseases.*[3]"

It was true, and I knew it. True hope has to be beyond this world, not in angels or demons who want gifts for themselves. And all my life I thought that everything bad came from the bad stuff I did in the life before, or that Papa did, or Yay and Da. Imagine power that is good?

I do not know how long we talked. But I left the riverfront with a peace and power I cannot explain.

He gave me some money for a romok home, and I took it with no shame. As the wind whipped my hair about, a million thoughts flew through my head. All upside down and now right side up, all the things that never made sense. All the times that Da said, "It's not right, little one."

Like when Chea Vichea talked, I felt powerful again, but this was different. More real. Actually, somehow, free.

---

1   Ephesians 2:8-9 NLT
2   Ephesians 1:18 NLT
3   Luke 9:1 NLT

The romok rumbled and bumped down the dirt road, and I looked at my feet, bloodied and numb from the seven kilometer walk in my flip flops. We passed the school yard and the temple gate. The sky was deepening with the threat of a storm, and as I searched the road ahead for the cracked Angkor Beer sign just before the fish market, I sensed the spirits hanging there. I paid the driver and limped from the market towards my house. But rounding the corner at Uncle Heang's house, I caught sight of a crowd. My heart sank and I knew the spirit had Mama again.

The October sky gets dark around 4:00 p.m., so I realized that many hours had passed since I'd starting walking at dawn. When I saw Mama there, with the men holding her down, I felt no fear or dread. Only sadness. And then I remembered the words he had shown me. *"When the seventy-two disciples returned, they joyfully reported to him, 'Lord, even the demons obey us when we use your name!'*[4]*"*

I was a disciple of Preah Jesu, as of that very day. I told the demon to leave, just like the seventy-two. Her body lay still, and I dropped my head to rest expecting her to crumple into exhaustion and sleep.

But she practically leapt up, "Kunthea! What did you say to make it leave? What did you *do*?" Mama was wide awake, and she firmly grabbed my arm.

The room was full, but in that moment, it was just me and Mama. "Mama, today I met the God who has more power than all gods. He has power even over evil spirits, and his name is Preah Jesu. I told the spirit to leave in the name of Preah Jesu. It is this God's power that made the spirit leave." Then, for a scary moment, expecting the spirit

---

4   Luke 10:17 NLT

to grab me, choke me and scream, I instinctively pulled away, "Mama, what is wrong? You, you are not sleeping."

Mama pulled my face right up to hers and whispered, "Then this will be my God too."

And I knew then — it was gone. I knew then that the words in his book were true. That evil spirits flee away at the presence of Preah Jesu. She wept and held me tight, tighter than ever. My head fell to her breast and we both cried. The room fell silent for a long time it seemed. The late afternoon sun had pierced through the storm clouds and rolled in through the west window. And one by one I caught their eyes: Yay, Mr. Vuen, Uncle Heang, Aunt Mony, Sopheak, Sela and the twins. No one said a word, but the sun caught their tear-stained faces and glistened with hope. For the first time in months, I slept well. And the spirit never came back.

February 19, 2005
Twenty-three years old

Mama is so weak. But she reads her *Preah Buntuel* all the time. She reads well into the night waiting for Sokaa to come home. I see a tear on her face and, somehow, I know it, that Mama will die. I remember when Sina was born, how we thought she would die then. There was no hope then. Now Mama is so weak and yet so ready to leave this world and rest with her Preah Jesu. Most of our village knows it too. They whisper when we walk by, some with eyes that pity and some with eyes that judge. I am learning not to be angry. The eyes that pity and judge are also held in bondage.

"Only by dying could he break the power of the devil, who had the power of death. Only in this way could he set free all who have lived their lives as slaves to the fear of dying.⁵"

March 27, 2005
Twenty-three years old

Pastor Vanna heard about a job with an NGO that teaches health to kids in villages. He knows I am not afraid of speaking in front of crowds, so he told me about it. I did not know how I would tell Roath I was leaving the factory. We have been through so much together: the training, the marches, losing Chea Vichea. How many moments we shared, standing shoulder to shoulder in the face of angry factory supervisors and even military police? Together we were so strong.

Her eyes filled with tears, but she hugged me hard. "You have to do this for your family. Do not worry about me. We will keep standing strong, Kunthea, and we will never forget how strong you stood in the face of so much danger."

Someday I would tell Roath again that any strength I have is not from me. She still thinks that her good deeds are buying merit, and she does not want to hear about "the foreigner's God".

The job pays $80 a month and pays for my lunch. I promised Roath that I will keep meeting with her outside of worktime, so we meet for breakfast sometimes early on Sundays at the Wat Phnom circle.

The twins are old enough to work now, at another factory. But Mony is so lazy, she got fired. I told her she must do the washing and cleaning at home if she is not bringing income to our family. No one

---

5   Hebrews 2:14

wants her to cook. We all get sick. I know from the health lessons that she contaminated our food by using the river water. She was too lazy to boil it. Sokaa has a job too, but he only makes $50 a month, and I am afraid he will not keep it since he is getting drunk all the time. Some months we never see any of that $50.

July 11, 2005
Twenty-three years old

My old friend Vuthy from the shoe factory came to see me today! I cried when I saw her, because I had no idea if she was even ok. And she cried too. She held me tight and tried to talk, "I did not know how to find you." But she did, and that is all that matters. It had been nine years. We were just girls at the shoe factory. I did not tell her what happened, only that I had to quit. It is hard to believe that I have been working for all these years. It makes me feel old, and I am only twenty-three.

August 18, 2005
Twenty-three years old

There are six people on our team of health educators. The NGO is French, and the boss does not speak Khmai, so he does not really know what Kinac is saying. I wish I could speak French. I'd tell him that his translator is lying to him. I'd tell him that his translator who bows in respect and uses sweet words with him says inappropriate things to me all the time. There are two problems between me and Kinac: one, the boss wants me to lead the teaching, and he is jealous, and two, he looks me up and down, all the while smiling and adding sugar to his tone so the boss does not notice. If he knew I was ruined, he wouldn't want to have me.

October 21, 2005
Twenty-three years old

Yesterday I met Roath for breakfast again at Wat Phnom. There is a boy there, about sixteen years old, who makes food and sells it with his mom. They have the best food cart at Wat Phnom, so they are always busy. He also has the biggest smile, and people like that too. It is a family business, and his yay sits there by the cart, telling everyone what to do, since she is a bit old to do it herself. I can tell he loves his yay by the way he treats her. Real respect and love, not the kind you muster up because you have to. Right then, as we waited in line at their cart, the smiling boy just stopped and stared with his mouth hanging open. Suddenly, there in front of everyone, a monk was on his knees on the dusty ground there by the cart, bowing all the way to the dirt in front of the boy's yay, crying! Imagine that!

Then his mama put her hands over her face and slumped onto a plastic chair. We were all just standing there with our mouths hanging open when the boy suddenly realized there was a line for his food, and he began dumping the hot noodles into bowls for the customers. But he was so distracted he forgot to take money, and we needed to pay still. The silence of the small crowd was magnified by the strange sobbing babble of the monk. Feeling like we had just walked into someone's private life, I motioned to Roath and we walked away and sat on the curb to eat our noodles. But we did not talk. We just kept listening but trying not to look.

"My brother!" And then she said that two more times, getting louder and louder, before breaking down into sobs while her son held her. "All these years we thought he was dead!"

Roath and I walked farther away. We would ask the boy another day. I looked back and saw the morning sun bouncing off the monk's dirtied orange robe and his shaven head, as he just kept bowing at the feet of the old woman, until she slumped over and fell off her chair, as another young man caught her in his arms.

November 1, 2005
Twenty-three years old

I remember the first time I thought Mama would die — when she gave birth to Sina. That was eleven years ago. This time she really will, and I do not know what I will do. I will be a very young mama to my siblings. Sopheak is already their papa, and the weight of it is so very heavy.

December 4, 2005
Twenty-three years old

Today was my breakfast date with Roath again, and the smiling noodle cart boy told us what happened. It was a slower day and he had time to talk. Also, he is not shy at all, so he told us the whole story! The monk was his uncle, the uncle they all thought was dead from the Pol Pot time. For twenty years his yay thought her son to be dead. She'd stopped wondering if, perhaps, he had lived. He had escaped into Thailand and, believing his family to be dead, eventually became a monk there. I thought about my mama's lost brother, the one Da called "the other one," the one I imagined coming home and standing in Da and Yay's doorway. This is the story that came true for the noodle boy's yay, and I was happy for them.

He explained, "There he was, all these years in Thailand, not knowing who in his family was dead or alive, and he was listening to the radio. He remembered that his family were musicians and song-writers, and he heard a voice that he knew, singing. And the announcer said, 'The song was written and sung by Dy Seng Bun,' his cousin, my uncle! On the day you saw him bowing at the feet of my yay, his mama, he had travelled on foot, through the whole night, to be reunited with his family. He is my uncle, and I never knew him."

The noodle boy got tears in his eyes then, and he turned to wipe his face in his krama. I touched his shoulder. "Thank you, *b'oan,* younger brother, for sharing your joyful story with us." I wanted him to know there is no shame in crying.

December 19, 2005
Twenty-three years old

Her thinned hair was moistened with sweat, as one who struggled, but her face was full of peace. And I knew that I'd never have to see my mama cry again. No tears of worry when Sokaa did not come home. No tears of shame when Mony lost a job. No tears of anguish for the pain of her children.

We gathered around her body as her soul slipped away to be with her precious Jesu. It was 11:20 p.m. and we did not call the monks because we knew where Mama's spirit was. She was not cold, naked, hungry or angry. She was complete and at rest. As the candles burned to small stumps, we sang quietly around her body. Aunt Mony and Uncle Heang helped us wrap her body. I took the wedding portrait off the hut wall and propped it up at her feet. Sela found some bougain-villea and made a wreath of it.

It was not like Papa's funeral. It was just our family, and a few others. Sotheary and her aunt Tata came, and two teachers from the school. Perhaps the rest were afraid of Mama's spirit. Perhaps they only remember her when the spirits controlled her.

I knew it was coming, because Mama knew. Last week she gath-ered us together and said, "Listen well. You will have many choices, but there is only one to make. Follow Preah Jesu no matter what happens." Then she told us her favorite stories from the Bible. "Listen, these are not just sayings or ideas. They are true."

Normally Mama was so weak, barely able to lift her head out of the hammock. But then, when she talked about Jesu, with her children gathered round, she had energy and excitement.

"The rich will not be rich in the afterlife because of being good, and the poor will not be poor because of being bad. Oh no!" And she told us the story of the rich man and Lazarus. Lazarus was a sick beg-gar who sat by the gate of the rich man, hoping he would share some morsel of his leftover food. But the rich man looked down on him and never shared. Then Mama told us that the when they both died, the rich man went to the deepest hell, and Lazarus went to be with the God above all gods, where there was peace and joy forever.

Me and Sopheak and Sela knew that story already. But the twins and Sina had never heard it. Their mouths gaped open at the thought, and their eyes popped wide. The stories of the Bible turn all the ideas we had before upside down.

And I sat thinking about all the times I heard Da say, "It's not right, little one!" I knew deep in my heart he was right. God takes the darkness and makes it into light.

Then I noticed Sokaa. He just stared at the floor, trying his best to respect Mama by staying in the room. But he could not get past his anger to see the truth. Mama saw him too, and she glanced my way and smiled softly. She was not worried, so neither was I. One week later, she was gone.

March 20, 2006
Twenty-four years old

It has been three months since Mama died. Since Mama and Papa had government jobs, we still got $50 a month as long as they were alive. Now we just do not have enough.

Last week we ate nothing but a spoonful of rice each for three days, and then nothing for four more. On the second day, we decided to sing and praise God for all we had. And each day after, when the hunger pains came, we sang some more.

The neighbors laughed, "Where is your foreign god now? See what happens when you disregard the spirits? Your mama and papa are angry! They are hungry ghosts with disrespectful children. You shame them!"

But we knew it was all lies, and by the fourth day we were no longer hungry! We sang and read, and the Words of God became our food. Even Sokaa could not deny it. Our God is the God above all gods.

"Gather together and come, you fugitives from surrounding nations. What fools they are who carry around their wooden idols and pray to gods that cannot save! Consult together, argue your case. Get together and decide what to say. Who made these things known so long ago? What idol ever told you they would happen? Was it not I, the Lord? For there is no other God but me, a righteous God and Savior. There is none but me. Let all the world look to me for salvation! For I am God; there is no other. I have sworn by my own name; I have spoken the truth, and I will never go back on my word: Every knee will bend to me, and every tongue will declare allegiance to me." The people will declare, 'The Lord is the source of all my righteousness and strength.'[6]"

July 2, 2006
Twenty-four years old

Pastor Vanna talked to me after church today, "Kunthea, I see how you study the scriptures and how God gives you understanding. I have a scholarship for one year at the Bible school. Do you want to go?"

Sopheak has a better job now, so he told me I should go. I'll have to go live in the dorm there. I am worried about the children, but we have decided I should go.

September 14, 2006
Twenty-four years old

It is hard to keep up with my studies. I have not spent much time reading all these years, so I am very slow at it. But I love it. Every day my world keeps turning upside down and right side up, out of bondage and into freedom. Every day I am walking out of darkness into light.

---

6   Isaiah 45:20-24 NLT

October 15, 2006
Twenty-four years old

Sela's small figure was leaning over me. "You have to breathe, *bong*! The pain will be worse if you don't." My sweet funny Sela was not laughing. Her wide-set soft-brown eyes were stern on her fairy-tale triangular face. She was scared for me, and not afraid to take charge. She was right — the tears were catching my throat so I held my breath. One in each of mine, I gripped both her hands hard, and vaguely heard Sopheak's voice at some distance, pleading, "Please . . . help my sister!"

I missed two whole days of classes as the pain came and went. It began at 5:00 a.m. and woke me up. It was on my right lower back and within an hour it was the whole right side. Sela used our market money to get a tuk-tuk and took me to the local public hospital. The October night rains had come so the road was flooded, and I could see the rippling muddy waters through the floor slats of the tuk-tuk in the dawn's light, as Sopheak held me up. Suddenly the tuk-tuk dropped hard into the broken road. The jolt was overwhelming and I cried out in pain. Sela slipped into Sopheak's place, as he leapt out and splashed into the murky floodwater, which was rising above the floor slats now. Voices calling out bounced about me. "Let me help! Come along, boys! One-two-three . . . Push!" The engine gargled and heaved with another painful thud, and Sopheak was leaping back in.

"Let's go!" I realize now that I actually saw very little of this since my eyes were shut tight.

We pulled in and there were others there waiting. No staff. I wanted to be brave but could not stop the tears from flowing, and others gathered around us to see what was wrong.

"Do you have any money? They won't see you without it." I rolled over so only Sela could see my face, and whispered through the tears, "Please just take me home. It's no use." The driver got out his hammock and tied it firmly across the tuk-tuk, and he and Sopheak lifted me into it. The pain got steadily worse and I thought I would die. I cried harder at the thought. How could I leave them when they have already lost Mama and Papa? Surely, Sela and Sopheak were thinking it, too. I could hear it in their desperate pleas, "Breathe, *bong*, breathe!"

From under the tuk-tuk canopy, I saw feet moving about. Dirty feet in broken flip flops. Bare wounded feet hobbling. White rubber clogs — a nurse. My eyes followed those feet to a nearby table. I saw her set a plastic bag on the table as she sat down. She would eat her breakfast while I die. The shame of being ignored was suddenly worse than the pain.

An hour later, they laid me on a mat-covered table, and a long time after that, someone gave Sela a tiny bag with two pills in it, while Sopheak dug three hundred riel from his pocket. When we got home, I heard the driver mumble, "My wife had that. It is a rock that comes into in the kidney. She needs to drink a lot of water. Clean water." Sopheak thanked him and glanced at me. We both grimaced, thinking, *We do not have much of that.*

I think pain like that makes you fearful or fierce. I pray it makes me both — fierce for all I am meant for, and fearful to know I cannot do it alone.

November 1, 2006
Twenty-four years old

My roommate, Srey Min, acts so respectful to the teachers' faces, but I see her roll her eyes when they are not looking. She also is not interested in talking with me. I wonder why she is at the school. We do not see each other much anyway, because I go back and forth so often. Sopheak is having a hard time with Sokaa and Mony. So, I go home to help him. I do not really have time to make friends at the school, because I have too many responsibilities at home.

February 20, 2007
Twenty-five years old

Today I was called to the school office. "Where do you go at night, Kunthea? Who are you with? We heard through the guard that one of the girls is pregnant. You have a scholarship and a safe place to stay!"

I felt sick and started to cry. How could they speak to me like this? "I go to help my brother with our siblings at home. Our parents are both dead."

Just then, Miss Sandra hurried into the room and she stood by me. She reached out and squeezed my hand. "Kunthea, please wait in the hall while we all talk." Her soft green eyes locked with mine as she walked me to the door. I paced the hall, thinking of all I'd been through, and all I was learning, and how none of this made sense.

The twenty minutes seemed like hours, and when they called me back in, the school head, Pastor Sar, apologized. "Kunthea, we are so sorry. Apparently, your roommate, Srey Min, is the one who is pregnant. She told the guard lies about you, to get the focus off of her."

I did not feel angry with Srey Min really. Just sad. She came to Bible School because she had been a translator for an Australian church that comes with short-term teams. They decided to sponsor her to go to Bible school. She agreed, even though she did not want to go. After all, she did not want to disgrace them by refusing the gift, and besides, it would mean a good job with an NGO someday.

When I got back to our room, she was gone, with all of her things.

August 20, 2007
Twenty-five years old

My Bible school year is over now, and I miss studying. But Sopheak's salary was not really enough so it is good I can work again. I got a job at a Christian hospital. They care for the poor, since they are rejected at the public hospital. What joy it gives me to help care for my own people there. Most of the staff are Khmai, and there are some Christian missionaries from other countries as well, but they speak Khmai. They speak with different accents — American, Australian, Korean and German — but most of the time we understand just fine! Working here helps me see that our God really is the God of all people from all nations.

I stood looking out at the small crowd. Young and old, they sat on the wooden benches awaiting my words. My heart was full of compassion as I saw their faces, travel-worn, sick and weary. They saw me standing there up front, and tried to sit up straight and be respectful, the way the Khmai poor do. It was overwhelming. I sucked in air and blinked hard. When I opened my eyes, I spotted a thin young man, my own age I think, sat hunched to one side in a wheelchair pushed by his papa or uncle. His gentle smile and tousled hair made me smile too and lifted me out of my fears.

"Welcome! We are so glad you are here. At our hospital, we respect and love all people, because we follow Preah Jesu, and He loves and respects all people, rich and poor, healthy and sick, and no matter your religion. We give everyone the same good medical care. Do not be afraid. You may have to wait while others who are worse off are seen first, but you will never be ignored, because Preah Jesu says in His words, that you have great value!"

It has been one month since I started working at the Christian hospital. I never know what the day will bring. Too often it is too late for their broken bodies, so we point them to heaven.

"Can anything ever separate us from Christ's love? Does it mean he no longer loves us if we have trouble or calamity, or are persecuted, or hungry, or destitute, or in danger, or threatened with death? (As the Scriptures say, 'For your sake we are killed every day; we are being slaughtered like sheep.' No, despite all these things, overwhelming victory is ours through Christ, who loved us.

And I am convinced that nothing can ever separate us from God's love. Neither death nor life, neither angels nor demons, neither our fears for today nor our worries about tomorrow—not even the powers of hell can separate us from God's love. No power in the sky above or in the earth below—indeed, nothing in all creation will ever be able to separate us from the love of God that is revealed in Christ Jesus our Lord.'"

---

7   Romans 8:35-39 NLT

September 15, 2007
Twenty-five years old

"Kunthea! There is an American man from a church in America. He has been asking about your family. Kunthea, I sent him a picture of you. He wants to marry you! Praise God, He is providing for your family! Look the man has sent some money and gifts already." I was stunned and just stared at her not knowing what to think. Changing her tone, she smiled, "Of course, he said to think and pray about it, and the gift is yours either way." I hesitated as she took hold of my hands and shoved the gifts towards me. Her voice became hard and low. Glancing around, she leaned in to me, "Don't be a fool, Kunthea. You are poor and the poor have no choices. He is coming next month. You will stay with him at a hotel." She handed me a gold necklace with a little cross on it, and an envelope.

When I handed the money to Sopheak, he held it to his chest and stared beyond me, out the window to where the sky glowed pink over the Mekong. He gulped and squinted his eyes. They were glassy with tears. We heard one of the children climbing the ladder, and he quickly stuffed it in his pocket.

In the night, I rolled over and over, not able to sleep. I heard Sopheak doing the same, from under the boys' net. My neck could not hold the weight of my head when I tried to lift it, so I turned onto my side and stared over at Sopheak. Did loving my family really mean I had to leave them? Is this man young or old? Does it even matter, if he will support our family? I felt so selfish for thinking about my own feelings. No one else would ever have me because I am ruined. But this American man . . . does he not care? Would I need not reveal my secret? Why did I think I could take care of my family with no husband? With no husband and a low paying job . . . Maybe they'd have done better without me. Maybe I should have tied Papa's krama to the rafters and hung myself after all.

Sopheak must have been thinking about it too. Seeing through the nets, his profile that used to be boyish seems suddenly manly, but with the worried lines of an old man. I caught the reflection of the moonlight in his eyes, and I heard him suck in his breath.

I awoke to his touch on my arm in the early morning dim glow, with my eyes stingy and puffed from crying myself to sleep. I slid my arm off of Sina and pulled up the red blanket to keep her warm. Crawling out from under the net, I could see it on his face. He had a plan. We climbed down the ladder and moved to the alley. He took my hands and whispered, "You need to talk with Mandy. She is American and she might have advice."

September 18, 2007
Twenty-five years old

We sat on her tile floor for almost two hours while I explained. She asked me many questions. When I told her that he wanted me to stay in a hotel with him when he comes, she looked out the window for a moment and bit her lip, as her light blue eyes filled with tears until they dropped. "Kunthea, some people in my country say they are Christians, but they are not walking down the road with Jesus. This man is one of those people." She also told me that it is against the law in Cambodia for a man who is over fifty to marry a Khmai woman who is under thirty. He is fifty-two, and I am twenty-five.

Meanwhile, Sopheak also talked with our American missionary friend, Sam. Sam boldly decided to call the man and get some facts. He is divorced. And he said he was not too concerned about Cambodian laws; he could just pay a bribe. When Sam tried to find out if he had any money, he got angry and hung up. Later Sam told Sopheak that not everyone in America has money.

The Buddhist proverb says that I am like soiled white cloth ... stained with the blood that ran down my legs. Ruined and never can be fixed. Never loved by a man. Never respected by anyone. But I read it in my Bible, upside down and right side up. I am washed clean, bright and white, like the snow from the pictures in Uncle Hak's magazines from Minnesota. He said it is soft, cool and refreshing. Not hard and clear like ice. But fluffy like the kapok in our pillows. But whiter, like the clouds! In Minnesota, they play in it and ride carts with no wheels but long thin smooth rods that glide through it, like Uncle Heang's fishing boat on the mighty Mekong. They fly like the wind, laughing and free. And the snow gives power to the moonlight, making even the darkness light and bright!

Sopheak and I decided I will not marry the American man. God has a better plan for me and my family. He has washed me white as snow.

December 2, 2007
Twenty-six years old

Today I found out that a human rights group made a video about Chea Vichea! Mandy told me about it; she has seen it! But we cannot buy it here in Cambodia, because it exposes some things, how they dragged in two innocent men. We all knew that they threatened to kill those guys' families unless they confessed. The video is called "Who killed Chea Vichea?" and someday I will get to see it.

CHAPTER TWENTY-EIGHT

Sophy

Sophy left her sunglasses on when she entered the shop. She knew her eyes were still puffy from crying the night before and had hoped to hide that from Phearun. He was busy talking with another customer, so she walked around the shop, looking at the books and straining to see the titles through the dark glasses. They had Christian Bibles, and New Testaments with Khmai on one side of each page and English on the other. And they had some children's books and translations of other works she had never seen before. In all her visits to the shop, Sophy had never taken the time to look and see what they had.

Sophy picked up the English-Khmai New testament Bible and tried to find some of Kunthea's quotes, but she didn't know where to look. Yet somehow, the familiar vocabulary was jumping off the pages at her. *Darkness. Light. Power. Love.*

"Can I help you, mam?" The customer had left and Phearun had walked up behind unnoticed.

"Oh, you surprised me!"

"Are you ok, Sophy?"

She took off the glasses, because it was no use. Sophy had one of those faces that held onto evidence of crying not only in the eyes. Her face got blotchy and even her lips got fatter.

"Well, a friend of mine left yesterday . . . unexpectedly. He was supposed to stay for another year, but he said . . ." The words caught in Sophy's throat and she couldn't finish.

"He said what?"

Sophy walked over to Phearun's desk and sat down. He took his seat as well, and leaned in across the desk, patiently waiting for an answer. Sophy's eyes began to fill again, and he gently pushed a roll of toilet paper towards her. She took the roll and unravelled a wad of tissue.

Sophy had found it amusing, the way the Khmai used toilet paper, not as toilet paper but rather as napkins and facial tissue. The bathrooms had sprayers, which were supposed to suffice. And for some reason all the water pressure seemed channelled to these sprayers so they were more like power washers. It had taken her two months to figure out how to use the sprayer without soaking her clothes and the whole bathroom.

She'd also learned that toilet paper does not make the best tissue for crying because it sticks to your eyelashes. As if her face didn't look bad enough when she cried, there would be little flecks of white toilet paper stuck all around her eyes.

She wiped her nose. "I am sorry to tell you, Phearun. But he said, 'This place is hopeless.' He meant Cambodia. You see, he was trying to help rescue girls because he really cares. But one of the girls chose to go back to her old life of prostitution, and it broke his heart. It really broke his heart, so he left."

Matthias had taken this internship in between undergrad and law school. He was heartbroken by human rights offenses: slave labor, trafficking, sweat shop factories. He had come to Safe Space as an undercover worker. He and a Khmai colleague would go to karaoke bars, posing as men who were looking for sex. They would meet the girls in the main bar area. When the pimps approached them, they'd feign interest in a certain girl, and then, they'd secretly offer the girl a way out. Lina was one of those girls, fourteen years old. Like a child playing dress-ups, she wore platform heels and too much makeup. When they'd first met, she would not let her eyes meet his. But she had saved the phone number and snuck away to call the next day. Once at the safehouse for only a few weeks, it was like she was getting her childhood back. Matthias and Sophy had watched her playing volleyball with the other girls. No makeup or heels. Just flip flops, jeans and a loose t-shirt. Her ponytail bounced as she leapt up for the ball, and her laughter filled the playground. Sophy had watched Matthias, watching Lina. His arms spanned the width of the office window as he held onto the decorative security bars, peering out at the playground. He'd taken a deep breath of satisfaction. "Yes!" He celebrated, "This is what it is about, Sophy. This is why I came. This is why I will study law."

He'd turned and looked at Sophy, his pale sapphire-green eyes penetrating into hers. "Sophy, there are so many Linas out there."

He was energized and motivated to find more Linas, until a few days ago. Lina left. She chose to go back. She said it was too late. She was already ruined and her family needed her to work. She would never make as much cutting hair.

Leaning back in his chair, Phearun paused and looked out towards the sun-filled courtyard near the front gate. After a while he said, "Sophy, can I ask you a question?"

"Sure, Phearun," she softly replied.

"What do you think? Is Cambodia hopeless?"

Elbows on the desk and head in her hands, Sophy could not look at Phearun while she said, "Honestly? I do not know what I think." Turning her gaze towards him, she went on, "I think I know what Kunthea would say." He waited for her to go on.

"She'd say that hope cannot be attained on our own. That it has to come from someplace bigger, beyond this world." Phrases from the diary flooded her thoughts, creating images. Images of despair and then of hope, and her heart bounced back and forth.

"I guess I have some things to figure out. Phearun, I did not know how to answer my friend. I also do not understand why Lina left. How could she choose that degrading life when she had tasted something far better?"

"Maybe you and she are defining 'better' differently."

Sophy's head hurt, pondering that thought. "Maybe defining 'better' is like defining hope. What do you think, Phearun? Is sacrificing her dignity for her family a good thing?"

"Well, I think survival plays a big role. But every culture has blind spots, and none of them have it completely right. You said that Kunthea would say hope has to come from something bigger than us, beyond this world. If that is true, then our human definitions are inadequate."

Sophy tilted her head and smiled at him. "Your English amazes me, Phearun. 'Our human definitions are inadequate.' My parents have lived in the US for thirty years and their English is terri — not good."

CHAPTER TWENTY-NINE

Thirty minutes later, she heard voices coming down the hall, speaking Khmai. Ali and another Khmai staff person emerged from the hallway.

"There she is!" Switching to his charming British English, Ali pulled up a chair and plopped a blue plastic sleeve on the desk. "Can we talk about this?"

"Sure . . . Please." Her blotchy face had cleared up a bit, so Ali did not notice and he jumped to the point.

"We are almost done. There are eleven entries left. You know how in that last set of entries Kunthea mentioned the first names of two foreigners, Mandy and Sam? I may know who Mandy is. This could go a long way towards us finding Kunthea to return the diary. Is it ok with you if I go ahead and try to contact Mandy? I know you are leaving soon, and it would be great if we can find a way to return it before you go." This was great news. Although she was glad she'd found the diary, she was also worn out by all the challenges it had given her, so much to think through.

Sophy nodded. "Yes. Please do, Ali. And . . . perhaps she could return it for us, so we'd stay anonymous. I just want Kunthea's story to be her own. Reading it has changed my life, but it is hers to keep. I just . . . Do you know what I mean?"

Phearun and Ali shared a smile. "Yes, we know what you mean. And we are glad this diary fell into your hands."

"Oh, and Sophy," Ali remembered, "the second notebook. It is not a continuation of her diary. But I do not want to ruin the surprise for you."

Sophy looked down at the folder she held. "Is it translated in here?"

"Yes. And it is brilliant," he beamed.

KUNTHEA'S DIARY PART SEVEN

January 15, 2008
Twenty-six years old

I am twenty-six years old. It has been twelve years since I decided not to kill myself, and thirteen years since the fire. Four years since Preah Jesu arrested the demons and turned our lives life right side up . . . and one year since I decided not to marry an old foreign man. One year since I decided I do not need a husband, because Preah Jesu loves me and my family more than any man ever could. And I am happy.

September 10, 2008
Twenty-six years old

They carried her through the gate and laid her on a mat in the shade of the big mango tree. In all my days, I'd never seen one so thin. I caught Mao's eye, and we both moved in and knelt beside her. He gently held her wrist, covertly testing her pulse while I asked, "*B'oan*, can you hear me?" She slumped in her brother's arms as he knelt behind her. At the sound of my voice she raised her head slightly, and I could see she had been a beautiful girl — high cheek bones and big round dark eyes. Her hair now thinned, short and matted with sweat and dirt from the tuk-tuk ride, she tried to smile at me, and I saw it. I imagined her whole and clean, even though I'd never known her before. Lifting her onto the gurney, Mao winced in surprise at the feather light weight of her body.

By 3:00 p.m., they had run all the tests and confirmed. She had cancer. So, we all met with the family to tell them the news. We are not able to treat most cancers, especially when discovered so late. They'd have to take her to the big public hospital. The tears began to fall and even our doctor got choked up as he explained, "We are so sorry." So, they decided. They'd take her home to die. Thirty-six years old with three small children. They were out of money. "We'd rather she die with dignity than be treated like dirt. And we just do not have the money."

October 20, 2008
Twenty-six years old

I feel like I am in school again. School, that I never got to finish. It is like breathing fresh new air after the rain!

I get to use what I am learning every single day. Every Friday I study with Miss Moriah. She is a missionary counsellor who is training several of us at the hospital. I will never forget the tears in Miss Sophia's eyes when I told her I had to quit school. She said she knew this day would come. "You are so smart, Kunthea!" I wish she could see me now and know that I have not stopped learning.

November 1, 2008
Twenty-six years old

Dr. Trent came to find me. "Kunthea, we have run all the lab work and examined her thoroughly. This woman has nothing wrong with her medically. I think there is something going on in her life that is causing her stomach pain and racing heart. Can you meet with her?"

I listened as she explained, "A woman came to our village in a car and started walking around talking with people. When she stopped at my hut, she talked to my daughter who was hanging the laundry. When

I asked what she wanted, she said she was just passing through and asked where to buy bottled water. One week later, she came back and wanted to meet with me. She said there is a Chinese man who wants a wife, and that he would pay $2000 . . ." She stopped talking just then, swallowed hard and looked out the window, pushing her bunched up krama to her face.

I had learned from my factory union days: "*Ming*, I do not think he wants to marry your daughter. I am sorry to say he would want to sell her for sex." She broke down sobbing, and I held her hands in mine.

She choked out, "I knew in my heart something was wrong, but the money was so much and we have debts!" We talked a long while more, and then I asked her if I could pray for all of her needs and debts.

She decided then that she would not let this happen. I walked her to the gate, and she hugged me and left with no words, just tears. I stood there in the late day sun and watched her wrap her hair up under her krama and toss the one long end up over her shoulder so it covered her mouth from the road dust, exactly the way Mama used to. She glanced back at me one more time. Mama used to do that too. And I prayed again on my own, that Preah Jesu would take away her family's hunger, like He did for mine.

"Then when you call, the LORD will answer. 'Yes, I am here,' he will quickly reply. "Remove the heavy yoke of oppression. Stop pointing your finger and spreading vicious rumors! Feed the hungry, and help those in trouble. Then your light will shine out from the darkness, and the darkness around you will be as bright as noon. The LORD [will] guide you continually, giving you water when you are dry and restoring your strength. You will be like a well-watered garden, like an ever-flowing spring[8]."

December 14, 2008
Twenty-six years old

My best friend at the hospital got married! Reaksmey works in physiotherapy. Her papa has been so sick with the sweet urine disease, diabetes, the same illness Papa had. One week before the wedding, he was in our hospital and we thought he would die, but he made it! He has diabetic foot problems and his feet are so bad he could not even wear his sandals in the wedding. So, there he stood, in his dress-up suit, on his naked stubble feet, proud of his little-girl-grown-up, as she and Vibol made their special vows. It was amazing, the first Christian Khmai wedding I have seen, all the beauty of a traditional Khmai wedding that I have loved since I was little: the matching beaded silks, the colors, the puffy flowing tent, even the comedian show. But no chanting monks trying to ward off evil spirits. No unhappy bride wondering if she would ever learn to love him . . . or wishing against all odds that he'd be faithful. As their voices lingered in sweetness, my thoughts drifted with the breeze, into the pink and gold tent billows. I was dreaming of such a love as this.

---

8   Isaiah 58:9-11

January 16, 2009
Twenty-seven years old

Oh my, Reaksmey has been teasing me about meeting a man, a friend of Vibol's from Bible school. I think she dreams of me being married more than I do! I have been resisting. Today she sat down across the table at the hospital canteen and just boldly handed me her phone, with his Facebook profile up! How embarrassing! I rolled my eyes at her and handed it right back. She glanced around, leaned across the table and whispered, "What makes you think you don't deserve a man to love you?" It caught me by surprise, and my eyes got teary. She squeezed my hand and I quickly wiped my eyes as Mao and some of the other nurses joined us. She is right. I do think I do not deserve it. Or that I am unclean. Ruined. Why am I still believing the lies?

February 24, 2009
Twenty-seven years old

We have been writing back and forth on messenger; we can type the Khmai letters on there now. I heard people are doing it all over the world, in their own languages, on the new "smart" phones. I saved and got an old used one.

Tinak has two sisters and a mom. His papa died many years ago when he was little. I have never heard his voice, but I hear it in my own head: a gentle softness, low and firm, like unmovable house stilts, the kind made of stone and set deep in the ground, that would never burn in a fire or wash away in a flood.

He works for a Christian anti-trafficking organization doing undercover research to find traffickers. He and his work partner, they have to be like actors, pretending to want to pay for girls or pretending to help foreigners find girls . . . or boys. It is so sad. And I can hear it in his voice — the compassion and passion to see people set free from evil. He also knows it's not right.

He listens when he writes. He wants to know me. Me . . . Kunthea . . . who has responsibility for many siblings. Kunthea, who never finished school. Kunthea, who has a secret too big to tell.

I can hear my heart beating as his words pop up on my screen. And I cannot keep from smiling in anticipation of his next words. And they just keep getting sweeter. Not the fake sweet words with sugar dusted on top, but the real kind. I know the difference.

But I felt uneasy about continuing to text with him without discussing it with Sopheak. Sopheak is the father of our household since Papa died. We have been through so much together and he has wisdom from God for our family. I have watched him agonize over many decisions. And he would not even think of marrying himself until he found good husbands for Sela, Malia and Mony. "I have a plan, Kunthea. I will send each of the girls to Bible school for the one-year program. They will learn the words of *Preah Awng* and I will pray that they meet a good man who follows *Preah Jesu*."

And his plan worked! At Sela's wedding, I watched my brother carefully observing a girl from Sela's husband's family. But he patiently waited until all three of them were married. Sina is still young and she is caring for Yay and Da. Finally, he felt free to marry, too. There is no one else whose blessing means so much to me.

"Kunthea, you think I am the head of our family, but where would I be without you?" Sopheak leaned in and tears filled his eyes. "You meet him in person first, and then if you want to move forward, we will set a time for me to meet him."

March 3, 2009
Twenty-seven years old

"I know why my son is sick, *b'oan srey*. It is because there is a curse on him. But I cannot tell the doctors that! They will never believe me. Especially the foreign ones. " I asked the patient's father to explain more.

"You see, my father was killed when I was fourteen, in the fighting after Pol Pot times when there was still fighting. One week after he died, I went with my mother to the spirit teller. He called up the spirit of my father and began to speak exactly in my father's real voice. First, he told us about things that would happen to us in the future, and then he told us where he had hidden money under our house. We found the money just where he said, and now the other things are happening too, including this. My child is sick."

The fear in his eyes gripped my heart. "I thought because he was grown we had escaped the curse." He began to weep.

I explained that our doctors will believe him, even the foreign ones, because they follow the road of Preah Jesu, who has authority over all the spirits. And then I got to tell him my story, Mama's story, our story. And I realized, it was the first time in a long time. It was so good to remember.

March 30, 2009
Twenty-seven years old

The messaging was safe. Meeting him in person was not. My heart was racing and I prayed on the romok that I would be calm. We met on the riverfront. I knew his face from Facebook, the wide smile and curly thick black hair, but honestly, I thought he'd be taller. He was wearing blue jeans and a green t-shirt, and I was glad he did not get all dressed up. Like the sturdy stone stilts I'd imagined, his voice was low and firm but gentle. He bought us some pork dumplings and we sat on a bench, eating and talking. Three hours later, I saw my watch and was shocked. I did not know how the time went so fast! Talking with Tinak was so natural. But I knew the next time I'd have to tell him. He was getting serious about me, and I was falling for him like the rain on Da's tin roof — hard and strong and loud. And I wondered if he could hear it too.

April 15, 2009
Twenty-seven years old

Khmai New Year is in two days and Tinak is going to his home in the province. He wants me to go with him and meet his mama and sisters. So, I knew we had to talk. It made me nauseous, but I had no choice. No one but Mama knew, and she is gone. I could not go on without him knowing. The words just tumbled out of me, through tears. There he sat, straddled over the grey granite bench that lines the riverfront as far as you can see. There he sat, not next to me, but facing me. There he sat, his black eyes meeting mine. A tear dropped down his face and we both fell silent.

I looked out at the Mekong, this mighty river that has meandered through my whole life and thought. Here I am again, wondering what the next bend will hold. The cruise boat drivers were calling out for customers as tourists wearing elephant pants from the market strolled by with their cameras. Pigeons flapped their wings as they scrambled for strewn seeds. Land mine victims hobbled about with their dirty caps held out at each passerby, "*Soam m'roey.* Please, a hundred reil?"

I watched all of this thinking of nothing. No expectations, no plans for me — Kunthea. Isn't it enough, what I already have?

Suddenly, my hand was in his firm grip, and the warmth rippled through my arm and up into my face. I cast my eyes downward, and he softly placed his other hand under my chin, lifting my face to catch his eyes again. Not bothering to wipe them away, he softly smiled through his own tears, "Oan, don't you know that Preah Jesu has made you clean and new? That He always loved you, even before you loved Him? This is the Kunthea I see. Clean and new . . . and beautiful."

July 21, 2009
Twenty-seven years old

It was such a hard decision. I will have to quit my job at the hospital when we get married. I have dreamt for so long of being a real counselor. Maybe I can go back someday, but for now I will start my own business so he can go to school and study law. Mandy has a friend who has a sewing machine I can have, and we have enough saved between us to buy a washing machine. I will do a laundry and sewing service in my village. Then I will not have to have a moto or spend the gas money. We will have one moto for Tinak.

Sam and his wife have offered to be my parents in our wedding, so we can have a real ceremony. I never even thought I'd get married, and now a proper wedding with parents for an orphan. Imagine that? I thought of all the lies that I'd believed over the years, but still questioned in my heart. After Mama died, I'd hear their whispers as I walked to the market:

"Now she is an orphan . . . She will never be able to marry."

"Don't pity them; they deserve it. Bad karma."

August 1, 2009
Twenty-seven years old

"Let my teaching fall like rain, and my words descend like dew, like showers on new grass, like abundant rain on tender plants.[9]"

---

9   Deuteronomy 32: 2

THE SECOND DIARY

June 21, 2016

My mama gave me a writing book. It is called a diary. You write in it so you will never forget things that happen. She got it for me because she says I talk her ears off. Ha-ha, if I really did that Mama would not have to listen to my talking because she'd have no ears. Anyway, I will talk, and Mama will write. Even though I know my letters, I am not ready to write a lot. When I am bigger I will write myself, without Mama's help. She took me to the riverfront in the city, and we got ice cream and she bought me this diary. Then we sat on the river bench, the one that is so long you cannot see the end of it, and here we are! She also showed me her own diary that she started when she was five like me! So today I am writing in my diary for the very first time.

My mama's name is Kunthea, and my papa's name is Tinak. My name is Bopha, and it is the name of a beautiful flower. I am five now and my job is to play while Mama talks. But sometimes I listen. My mama helps the village women every day. She listens and prays and cries with them. And they read the words of Preah Jesu. But sometimes they whisper because some people hate us. Souphia will not be my friend anymore because her mama told her that we follow the foreigners' God and bad stuff will happen to her if she does. Souphia obeys her mama, but when I walk by her hut, she looks at me with really sad eyes. That makes my tummy hurt, and my heart too. Mama says we just need to pray for Souphia and her mama, so I do that every day. And I play with the kids so Mama can talk with their mamas. That is my job.

Our village is a fishing village with a fish market at one end. Mama has her own business right here in our village. And we live there in the green tin roadside shop: me, Papa and Mama. We sleep together on the big red flower mattress on the floor. I have a little round Hello Kitty pillow with a shiny pink ruffle around it. Aunt Sela gave me that. Mama and Papa got married one year before I was born. You have to get married before you have babies, or there would not be a mama and a papa to love them. That is the reason.

Aunt Sela lives with her husband in the one-wall bamboo house down the road, with my aunts and uncles. That is near the fish market. And at the other end of our road is the village market. Mama said it is a new market, because when she was a girl, the old one burned down. The whole village burned down because someone's mama and papa were fighting in their own grass hut, and they knocked over a lantern! That is why Mama is so careful about lanterns.

Papa says, when I was a baby, they put me in the hammock right over their bed, so whenever I started to cry like babies do, they could just swing me back to sleep.

At our green tin shop hut, there is one washing machine and two sewing machines for Mama's business, and one iron and one iron table to make the clothes look pretty. Mama says when I am big I can iron like Aunt Sela. Someday I will play with Souphia again, while Mama talks with her mama. It will happen.

Mama said that Papa decided to love her because Preah Jesu loves her. She thought she would never have a husband, but God gave her Papa. Now Mama works hard at the business so Papa can go to school. My papa is learning to be a law man. But he does not want to be a law man that takes bribes. He wants to be a law man who helps people with their problems, people like Sukia's papa. His land was taken away because the man next door is a big man with power. So, he just took it! And now Sukia and her mama and papa and all her sisters are sleeping under a blue plastic tarp behind their neighbor's hut, right on the ground with the rats and snakes! Sukia's mama keeps taking money to the ghost tellers and offerings to the temple. But her papa says it does no good; they just have bad karma from his life before. I heard them yelling at each other about that. Papa heard it too. He told me that the devil has told Sukia's family lies and they believe those lies. Papa saw my tears for Sukia, and he prayed with me. Someday, I will play with Sukia and Souphia while Mama talks with their mamas! It will happen.

One time, when Mama was young, she and Aunt Sela, Aunt Mony, Aunt Malia, Aunt Sina, Uncle Sokaa and Uncle Sopheak had no food! They decided to thank God for everything they did have! They sang the thankful songs, and guess what? They were not hungry at all, even though they had no food! Now if Preah Jesu loved them so much like that, I know He also loves Sukia and Souphia and their mamas and papas and brothers and sisters too! I know it.

Today I saw Papa watching Mama. He dropped a few tears over his smiling face. She was singing her favorite song.

"And every time I pray

Crooked paths are made straight

Mountains are removed

And nations turn to you."

My mama is beautiful, even when she cries. She sings like an angel from heaven. And when she sings that song, her tears fall. Mama says that those kind of tears are the kind that wash away everything sad and make us new, just like when the sky finally rains at the end of dry season and makes everything green again.

CHAPTER THIRTY

Sophy

Sophy sat sidesaddle on the back of Sret's 110cc moto, her yellow plastic disposable poncho only covered to her knees, leaving the bottom of her cropped jeans exposed and, by this time, completely soaked. Her hair was tied back under the plastic hood with her pink helmet smashed over that. Rain droplets flew past her from Sret's lime-green poncho as it puffed with the wind of the moto. Little rivers of windblown raindrops on her helmet visor blurred her view. She raised the visor with her free hand, trying to get a clearer view. *No windshield wipers on a helmet visor.* Her other hand held tight to the seat: she still could not imagine how the Khmai felt so at ease on the back of a moto that they did not hold on at all. And she thought, *So this is probably one of the things that makes people know I am not Khmai.* And she smiled remembering Sret's comment on that first day, "You look Khmai but you do not act Khmai."

Ali had finally heard back from Mandy. She was in the United States caring for a sick parent. She knew the name of Kunthea's village but had not yet been to the shop. He had pieced together the information and narrowed her location down to three streets in a certain fishing village on the Mekong, about thirty minutes outside the city. They knew from her daughter Bopha's diary it was a laundry and sewing shop, with green metal walls and roof. Sret had gone out on his own, combing the three streets for such a shop. He even asked some locals if there was a laundry shop nearby. And they had said, "Kunthea's place is the best. Next street over and about ten houses up by the coconut seller."

Ali and Phearun had agreed that Sophy should go on the secret mission to return the diaries. Since Mandy was in the United States, they'd made another plan. Sophy wanted Sret to take her, so she'd asked them if that was ok. "He has been a driver for Safe Space for years. He understands the importance of confidentiality. And he is just a really great guy." So, they'd invited him in and explained everything in Khmai. Ali and Phearun talked faster than she could follow, and Sophy watched in amazement, especially at Ali. He'd been in Cambodia over twenty years. He could joke, listen, and even empathize, really communicate at a heart level. These six months had shown her how insufficient her Khmai was.

She had asked Ali once how long he'd studied the language. "Your Khmai is amazing."

"Yes well, most mission organizations place a high value on language learning. Formal study is only two years, but it never ends. Speak it or not, it is quite obvious that I am not Khmai." He laughed.

Sophy chimed in, "Sometimes I wish I had pale skin and red hair like you. Then at least maybe they'd understand why I am different."

Sret was only a driver, and yet, Ali and Phearun treated him with such respect. Sophy was able to pick up enough language to know this. And she thought that even if she did not know the language, you could tell by the way they treated him. And she thought of the patients at Kunthea's hospital. Sret leaned forward, his elbows on his knees, as they explained about the diary, nodding his head. At times he teared up.

At one point he'd looked at her and said, "So this is the reason for all the questions!" And their laughter broke the weight of the moment.

CHAPTER THIRTY-ONE

"Well, Sophy, I guess this is goodbye," Phearun started, and Ali chimed in, "You will shoot us an email to let us know how it goes, right?" Sophy bit her lip and fought tears. She had never minded goodbyes before and was even a bit irritated by people who got emotional over them. Perhaps she'd never had a reason to feel truly sad about them. Perhaps she'd never let anyone get that close. Perhaps Kunthea had penetrated her veneer. Somehow it felt right, albeit hard.

"Of course, I will. And I want to say, thank you both, for all your help. You know, the diary, Kunthea, she kind of turned my life upside down. Thanks for taking on the project."

By this time tomorrow, she'd be on the plane home, to parents whose heritage she'd rejected. She'd spent her whole life embarrassed by them when she should have been proud. She kept playing the scene over in her mind. Her heart ached at the thought of seeing them at the airport in Cleveland. Not so much because she'd missed them these six months, but because she'd missed them her whole life. Missed who they really were. She grieved the pain her arrogance must have caused them. She knew she'd never be the same. She now knew that there was much she didn't know. She knew that the most important things she was learning had nothing to do with university degrees. And she knew she still had a lot to figure out. What she'd anticipated for this internship and what she got were two very different things.

And now the time had come. They motored up the narrow road in the gently falling rain. Sret parked the bike at the open-air noodle shop and sat at a metal folding table near the road, facing Kunthea's laundry shop across the road, five short meters away. Like most shops in Cambodia, the fronts were completely open, with top-down rolling gates to shut them off at night. Some had decent awnings in striped vinyl that rolled in and out. Some had permanent tin awnings, but most had home-rigged tarps or fabrics propped up on rickety bamboo poles. Sophy had been intrigued by how this open-air commerce added to the communal feel. Walking down a Cambodian street was like walking through a row of temporary booths at a fair in Ohio, and walking *into* a shop did not involve opening any doors.

Sret sat next to her, and they ordered iced coffees. They did not say a word as they both gazed at the scene across the street. Under a blue plastic tarp awning sat a very old man in an old folding lawn chair that sat crooked. A blue *krama* was tied around his thin waist, and he wore worn green rubber flip flops on his stiffened grey feet. He had fallen asleep. Sophy's heart quickened when she saw a young woman walk out from the back of the shop with an armload of clothes. A little girl was marching behind her, with her own little load of clothes. Setting the load on a large cloth-covered table, she turned and took the girl's load, and kissed her on the head. Then another young woman emerged from the back with a small backpack on one shoulder. The two women chatted a moment, and the second woman took the little girl by the hand. She grabbed an umbrella in the other hand and popped it open as they ventured out onto the little broken concrete road. Out from under the awning, Sophy caught a clear look at her face — Sela.

She remembered Kunthea's description of her sister's triangular fairy-like face with wide-set eyes and the way she loved children and made them laugh. The rain still fell lightly and the little girl strayed out from under the umbrella, drawn to puddles along the way, where she stomped and splashed along in a sing-song sort of rhythm, with her silly aunt joining in. It was Sela and little Bopha. The one-walled house must be down the road that way, and Sophy found herself leaning forward, wanting to follow them.

CHAPTER THIRTY-TWO

Sophy's eyes returned to the first woman. But in the shadows of the tarp she was hard to see. The shop was like a cave, and since it shared walls with the one-room shop houses on either side, there were no windows. As her eyes adjusted, Sophy could make out the wall of the small room at the back — the same green corrugated metal of the shop, with one orange plastic door and a square cut-out window leading into the shop — the bedroom. A stream of light poured in from a narrow hallway to the left of the room, indicating a back entrance. The entire front room was no more than four meters wide and three meters deep. The young woman moved towards the front of the shop, under the tarp, and began to hang the wet clothes on hangers on a metal rack. Now nearer to the light of the open roadway, Sophy caught a glimpse of her face, and she was glad the noodle shop was busy, so no one would notice her staring. The young woman's long black hair was tied in a low ponytail that draped over her right shoulder in front. She wore cropped jeans, white rubber flip flops and a green t-shirt with white Khmai letters that read "*Timotay dti bi, bi:bi*", Second Timothy two:two, a Bible verse reference. This had to be her, Kunthea. Sophy's heart ached at *meeting* this girl she'd come to know over the last six months, but whom she had never actually talked with. Sophy felt grateful at that moment. Grateful for all she'd learned from the friend she'd never meet. And she wondered how you could feel you know someone so well when you'd never actually met.

Hanging the last shirt, Kunthea glanced at the old man and paused for a long moment and smiled. *Da*, Sophy surmised. *It must be her da.* She felt Sret's gaze and caught his eyes. She did not realize that she had let tears fall, and she saw the glassy reflection in his eyes too.

Sret — in these six short months, she'd glimpsed pieces of his heart. His sense of responsibility. His compassion. One day she dared to ask him what he remembered. He had been twelve years old during what he too called the "times of Pol Pot" and told her he remembered stepping on dead bodies to avoid landmines as his family trekked across the country. After he'd said that, he shook his head, looked away and stopped talking. She had seen those glassy eyes then as well, and Sophy began to understand why, sometimes, it was ok to not talk.

On another day, she'd asked him how he was doing, "*Sok Sabay?*"

"Oh, not good! I had a terrible dream last night. I was driving you and some of the girls in the old Safe Place Land Cruiser when the road broke up and we slid into a river! I had to save all of you as the car went under the water, but my clothes and shoes were so heavy. You were all crying out and I could not swim fast enough." He shook his head and took a deep breath.

Sophy knew that six months is not near long enough to know anyone, especially cross culturally, but she was grateful for the glimpses and what she had learned from each one of the Khmai people she'd worked with.

Sret nodded towards her bag, and Sophy knew the time had come. She lifted a small plastic bag out of her pack and pulled out two books: Kunthea's old worn diary and the new one of her little girl,

Bopha. He gripped the two books in his strong hands, and they waited until Kunthea went to the back of the shop. Sophy's heart raced as Sret sauntered across the tiny street. He laid the books on the folding table at the front of the shop, while glancing at the old sleeping man. As he jogged back to the noodle shop, the rain began to fall hard. Sret leaned on a metal poll at the front of the noodle shop, as he and Sophy each peered from their own positions. As the rain grew to a roar on the tin awning above them, Sophy saw Kunthea emerge through the misty veil. The steady sound drowned out all the other noises. No roosters crowing. No motos beeping. No dishes clanking. So that Sophy felt that she was watching a silent movie.

Kunthea saw the books immediately and snatched them up, turning to her da, who was still sleeping. The diaries clutched to her chest, she ran first to the south corner of the propped-up blue tarp awning, scanning the little road for anyone who may have held, read and returned her secrets. Seeing no one suspicious, she pushed the rolling metal drying rack back into the shop. She stood right at the edge of the falling rain, straining to see any signs to the north. Then running right along the edge of the awning, splashing through the little river that had formed there on the road, she stuffed the books under her t-shirt and stared right across the street, straight at Sophy! Sophy slid her iced coffee towards her on the table, grabbing the tall spoon. Looking at it now, she realized that she never even remembered the server bringing it, and that the ice had already melted, leaving a layer of clear water on top of the dark coffee that topped the thick white layer of sweet milk on the bottom. Stirring her coffee, she glanced at Sret who was still leaning on the pole and gazing at the scene across the way. The bouncing light of the falling rain reflected off his face, which was stained with a tear. She bit her lip, and turned her eyes back towards Kunthea, who had fallen to her knees, books to her chest and face turned upward, smiling through her tears. Sophy thought of all the tears Kunthea had cried.

She listened to the sound of the falling rain, and it seemed like a new kind of beautiful music — the sound of everything being made new.

— THE END —

AFTERWORD

Fall like Rain is based on the true story of a Cambodian woman whose name has been changed in order to protect her privacy. A few of the events in the character's life are stories of other Cambodians. Details about life in Cambodia were filled in through extra characters and scenes. All stories about the Khmer Rouge genocide are true, as told by participants and eyewitnesses whom the author knows. The assassinations of both Chea Vichea and Kem Lay are true historical events, and the dates coincide correctly.

Sophy and her friends are fictitious characters, based on several people the author has met. Safe Space is a fictitious organization, based generally on similar organizations.